D1460167

DRAGON HEIR

THE HIDDEN KING TRILOGY

JEN L. GREY

Copyright © 2021 by Grey Valor Publishing, Inc

All rights reserved.

No part of this book may be reproduced in any form or by any electronic or
mechanical means, including information storage and retrieval systems,
without written permission from the author, except for the use of brief
quotations in a book review.

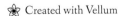 Created with Vellum

CHAPTER ONE

A few tears dripped down my cheeks as I stared at my fated mate in his angry dragon form. Smoke trickled from his nose, and his large, dark-olive-scaled body shook with rage. The cabin wall he'd barged through still rattled from the force. He was easily as wide as the cabin and extremely strong.

Ollie dug the knife in deeper against my neck. More blood poured from my wound, down my neck, and into my dark brown hair. Between the blood loss and the deep stab wound in my calf, my head swam. Knowing how to connect with my dragon would've come in handy, but it didn't matter.

I'd soon be dead.

Do not close your eyes, Egan said sternly. *Stay with me.* Fear permeated the bond.

I tried to force my eyes to stay open, but I was so damn tired. I had no clue why the falcon shifter was helping Vera, not that it would make a difference. Once Ollie slit my throat, keeping my eyes open wouldn't help. My eyelids fluttered as my dragon surged forward in a last-ditch effort to save us. She lent me her strength to tighten my hold on the bracelet I'd yanked off Vera. I muttered in barely a whisper, "Ollie, please. Stop. You don't have to do this."

The words slipped from my lips, even though it was a waste of energy.

Desperation slammed into me as Egan threw his head back, letting flames burst from his mouth. He charged toward me like he could prevent Ollie from finishing the job.

I closed my eyes, unable to watch Egan's reaction as I died. Even in death, that last look would haunt me.

I tensed, prepared to meet my end, when the knife clanked to the floor and Ollie's arm slackened. His body sagged, and I slipped from his arms. Too late, he reached for me like he realized what had happened. Unable to support my full weight, I sank toward the floor.

Egan dropped beside me, splitting the floor from his weight, and I landed on his neck instead of on the hard floor. I couldn't have survived another blow, so he'd bought me a little more time, but I wasn't sure I wanted it. The pain was all-consuming.

Car doors slammed shut outside, and Ollie sprang into action. He stumbled backward on his lanky legs, trying to get clear of us, his hands raised in surrender. His golden-brown hair stood almost straight up in fear.

"Do smthng!" Vera barked loudly despite her broken jaw and being so small. Her sable eyes were nearly black, and her stringy, caramel hair stuck to her face. "Kll hr!" she screamed barbarically.

Footsteps hit the ground as Sadie and the others ran straight to us through the completely destroyed wall. Arms slipped around my waist, and someone tugged me away from my mate. I wanted to yell and scream. I needed to be with him.

It's Sadie, Egan reassured me as he climbed back onto his feet, his attention locked on the falcon and the witch. *Let her take care of you while I handle them. I'll be right back.*

The comforting scent of musky vanilla hit my nose, confirming that it was her. They'd all come for me, and it meant more to me than I could ever say. I didn't see how I would come out of this alive.

Sadie was the next person I felt safe around. Since my dad's death, I hadn't felt secure and protected until I'd stumbled upon Egan and Sadie just over a month ago.

I smelled Donovan's and Axel's musky shifter scent as they rushed past me to fight alongside Egan. From where I sat, I watched Donovan grab Ollie by the throat and lift him into the air.

"Please don't," Ollie cried. "The witch was controlling me. I didn't have a choice but to hurt her."

"You expect me to believe that?" Donovan yelled, the vein between his brows popping. "Do you not realize how important she is to us?"

I startled at Donovan yelling, causing my leg to jerk, and I groaned in pain. I'd never experienced such agony before, not even after Aunt Sarah's worst beatings. Between the dizziness and nausea, I wasn't sure how I hadn't projectile-vomited yet.

"I'm telling the truth. Jade clawed the bracelet Vera was using to control me off the witch and told me to stop." Ollie pointed at me with a shaky finger. "Why else would I let her go, especially with you all charging at me?"

"Roxy, help me get her on the couch," Sadie said. Hands picked up my legs as Sadie adjusted her grip on my arms. "Lift her on the count of three. One ... two ... three." They picked me up, and I cried out in pain.

Just hold on a little longer, Egan pleaded as he hissed at the witch.

"Let's get you situated so we can check you over," Sadie said calmly, but the pain overwhelmed me, and my head grew light.

They slowly carried me over to the dirty old couch that had definitely seen better days. A cloud of dust covered me, tickling my nose.

"Shit," Roxy huffed and let go of my leg. "This isn't good."

Sadie's eyes landed on my leg, and she went still. "Lillith! Katherine!" Sadie shouted. "She's lost a lot of blood. We need your help." Worry filled her light blue eyes, and her rose-gold hair hung in her face as she stared down at me. Her usually sun-kissed skin appeared as pale as the vampires'.

The floor shook with each step Egan took as he charged after Vera. I really hoped he made her hurt like I was hurting. She enjoyed the pain she'd caused.

The crackling sound of fire hit my ears, and the smell of brimstone filled the cramped space. Normally, I would have lifted myself to check on him, but it was hard to even breathe.

"We have to move fast." Roxy ran her blood-coated hands through her red hair. Even with the scarlet color of her hair, the blood was noticeable. Her hazel eyes had lost their usual smart-ass sparkle.

"You kidnapped her back at the restaurant, right under our noses." Donovan sounded as scary as Egan. "Did you actually think we'd let you walk away?"

The witch had looked distraught when I'd taken the

bracelet, and the clasp had been sturdy. Maybe Ollie was telling the truth. "Bracelet," I mumbled and tried to raise my hand, but I couldn't. My eyelids were too heavy to keep open.

I wanted to stay conscious, but the world was fading along with the pain. The reprieve, even for a little while, would be a godsend. I didn't want to fight the darkness anymore. Sounds began to fade as loud footsteps rushed over to me. The vampires' signature scent of cotton candy alerted me that one of our friends had neared the couch.

A hand turned my head toward the vampire hovering over me. Something warm and thick pressed against my lips and dripped into my mouth. I wanted to pull away, but then my taste buds went crazy. I sucked hard, pulling more of the substance in. It tasted like rocky road ice cream.

Within seconds, my body felt stronger, and the sharp throbbing in my leg receded. I opened my eyes and found Lillith's wrist against my mouth.

No way. She wasn't feeding me her blood.

I jerked back and wiped the excess blood from my mouth as it trickled from the wound on her wrist to the ground.

"What the hell?" They could've warned me first.

"You needed healing." Sadie brushed my hair out of my face. "Vampire blood does wonders even if the thought is a little unappealing. You would have died otherwise."

Egan turned to me, his focus drifting from the witch. *Are you okay?*

Yeah, I assured him. "Her blood tastes good." That couldn't be normal. I sat up and lifted my pant leg. My wound had stopped bleeding and was already scabbing over. Considering how bad it had been only seconds ago, that was a miracle.

"Please," Ollie whispered. "I didn't want to hurt her."

Everything around me came back into focus. Killing Ollie would be a mistake if what he said was true. As long as we had the bracelet, we could control him and get whatever information we needed from him. But first things first.

"Thank you." I smiled at Lillith and climbed to my feet. Even though I felt immensely better, I still was a little woozy.

"You're not completely healed." Lillith looked paler than normal, and her jet-black hair and dark brown eyes surrounded by the dark red ring contrasted against her skin more than usual. Her all-black clothing added to the creepy effect. "So take it easy."

I linked with my mate. *We all know he's telling the truth.* I opened my hand, revealing the bracelet. The tarnished silver and strangely clear, quartz-like crystal with flecks of ash shone in the light. "We'd know if he was lying."

As I turned to Egan and Vera, the witch vanished into thin air. How the hell had she done that?

"She just disappeared." I pointed excitedly over to where she'd stood. Even though Egan had used his flames, nothing was on fire. He had to be able to channel it perfectly; otherwise, the cabin would've been up in a blaze.

Donovan dropped a purple-faced Ollie and scanned the room. "Where the hell did she go?"

Axel rushed to where she'd been and sniffed. "It's like she was never here. I don't smell a trail leading out the door."

A car started outside, and the tires squealed. I ran to the window and saw her speed down the gravel driveway.

Roxy ran to their car.

"Dammit," Axel grumbled and ran after his mate. Roxy jumped into the driver's seat, and Axel got into the passenger seat. She lurched the car into gear as she chased after the witch.

"Where is the witch going?" Donovan demanded as he turned back to Ollie.

The poor guy lifted his hands and averted his gaze to the ground. "I ... I don't know. She didn't tell me anything."

"Why should we keep you alive?" Sadie asked in a calmer but deadlier voice.

For the first time, I saw the true supernatural side of her, and she was a force to be reckoned with.

"Look, I swear." Ollie looked at me. "She told me what to do and who to attack." He gestured at the bracelet in my hand. "The black ash is from my scorched feather. She performed a spell to control me. You can keep the bracelet until I can prove I'm trustworthy. Just please, let me live."

Only one thing could prove he was telling the truth. I held the bracelet and lifted my chin. "Ollie, pick up the knife."

"What?" he asked, but he bent down and picked it up. Fear filled his eyes as he held the handle firmly in his hand.

What are you doing? Egan asked as the smoke dissipated from his mouth.

Finding out if it's true. I lifted a brow, daring the falcon. "Cut your forearm until I say stop."

"Please don't." His voice shook as he obediently cut through his skin like it was a piece of paper. Blood poured from the wound, and he continued to press the blade down harder and harder.

No one would do that willingly. "Stop." I couldn't make him hurt himself too much.

"Thank God," he whimpered and dropped the knife.

Lillith marched over to the falcon shifter. "What was her end game? You have to know that much."

"She wants to find your thunder," I told Egan. She'd let me in on that secret.

"Yes." Ollie nodded. "At first, she had me attack random girls, hoping you would investigate and we could nab something of yours to track you. But we only got a few items that weren't really tied to you and couldn't provide the best locations. When she realized you weren't inclined to go home, she upped the game and had me kill girls she thought you were either interested in or who could be your potential mate."

"Like Amber." I walked over to Egan and leaned against him, brushing my fingers against his hard scales. "Either Ollie told her, or she thought you were dating her."

Egan leaned against my hand, and I felt a purring sound emanating from deep inside him.

"It was me." Ollie hung his head. "She commanded me to tell her anything I could get on him. Given how intimate Amber seemed with you, I thought we'd found something."

"So you killed her?" Even if he'd had to, he'd committed cold-blooded murder. I couldn't imagine the pain Amber must have gone through. "And all those other girls."

"Yes." Remorse poured off Ollie. "I hated it, and I'll never forgive myself, but I had no choice. Vera was convinced that if his mate or girlfriend was killed, he'd rush home to his thunder, and if we had the blood of a girl he was emotionally tied to, the locator spell would be that much stronger."

Katherine wrung her hands. "Anything you have a connection to would strengthen the spell."

Then it hit me and hard. I sucked in a breath and glanced at my leg. She'd wiped my blood on her jeans before she'd disappeared. "She has my blood."

We weren't safe. She could find us anywhere.

CHAPTER TWO

The room was silent as everyone took in my words. Vera having my blood was disconcerting.

"What do you mean she has your blood?" Katherine asked as she tugged on the ends of her long brown hair. Her matching-colored eyes, with red ringing the irises, looked at me.

"My leg wound." I lifted my leg and gestured to my black slacks. Blood had soaked into the material and still dripped into my already overfilled black dress shoes. "When she yanked out the knife she stabbed me with, she wiped my blood on her clothes. Can't she use that or anything else she might have collected from our dorm room to track me?" The supernatural world had so many rules and caveats. Being human had been a whole lot simpler.

We need to get you back to the dorms so you can rest. Egan was still tense from the fight.

That sounded like a good plan. I felt stronger, but I was still exhausted. At least, I could stand and hold my weight, but I was tempted to crawl onto that nasty couch and take a long nap. However, the witch was still out there, and we had to figure out what the hell to do with Ollie. Even if I could control him, I didn't want him leaving our sight.

"I wonder if Roxy and Axel caught up to the witch." I doubted they had. Vera had several minutes' head start, but the roads were free of traffic. Maybe they'd gotten lucky.

Sadie sighed. "They didn't catch up to her. They're actually on their way back. It's like she vanished again."

"Can a witch hide a whole car?" There was so much I had to learn, and after tonight, I needed to catch up.

Ollie shook his head. "She's powerful. She knows long-forgotten spells. It's the oddest thing. That's how she was able to trap me. I had no clue it was even possible."

"I wonder how she has so much knowledge." Lillith pursed her lips. "She must have a spell book."

The image of the leather notebook flashed in my mind. "I think I know how. She carries around a book she says was her grandmother's journal. Maybe it's her grandmother's spell book."

"You're right." Ollie rubbed his neck, still red from where Donovan had held him. "I've seen it too. It makes sense that she would keep it close, especially while using magic."

"Great, but how did she go undetected around us?" Donovan frowned and towered over Ollie and the others. "We should've smelled her."

"She knew who we were." Sadie rubbed her bottom lip with her thumb. "She probably used magic to conceal herself."

"That's why she was in our room so much." The more she was outside, moving around, the more magic she had to use to hide herself.

Can you get the car keys from Donovan? Egan shifted

away from me. *I'd like to grab the spare clothes from the back and change into human form.*

"Donovan, can I get the keys?" I lifted my hands, ready for him to throw them. "Egan wants to shift back." I wanted him to as well. I'd never seen him in his dragon form before, and it tugged at me differently. I always felt safe around him, but in this form, I had no doubt he could protect me from anything.

That was why I needed to learn to control my dragon. Maybe tonight wouldn't have been so bad.

"Sure." He lobbed them gently at me, keeping his focus on Ollie.

The only reasons Ollie wasn't dead or injured were because the witch had been controlling him and we had the bracelet in our possession. Still, I didn't trust him either, so Donovan's wariness made it easier for me to leave with Egan. "Come on. I'll get your stuff out for you."

The others stayed behind as Egan and I went to his Jeep. I opened the trunk and found two bags.

Mine's the one on the left. He pointed one long claw in that direction. *Can you hand me the clothes? I'll go into the woods and shift back real fast.*

Happy to help, I placed them in his large dragon hands. He hurried off, nearly taking down a tree to go hide somewhere. As his huge body shrank, magic crackled in the air.

Needing a moment to myself, I leaned against the Jeep and waited for him to return. The night was catching up with me, and I couldn't believe I'd survived. To think I'd gone to work tonight at Haynes Steakhouse, believing Egan was being overly paranoid because of the killings popping up on campus, and I'd come close to the same fate. I hated that I hadn't respected his wishes that I just quit, but even if I had, Vera would've used Ollie to attack me, so maybe getting the kidnapping out of the way had been a blessing in disguise.

Either way, I had a feeling that wasn't the last we'd seen of her. She had something against the dragons—wait, against us. I was a dragon shifter too even if I hadn't shifted into a dragon yet.

Footsteps drew closer, and my sexy mate stepped out of the trees. He was so gorgeous he took my breath away.

He approached me, towering over me by a foot, which was saying something since I was almost six feet tall. He was built like an MMA fighter, and his loose, hunter-green t-shirt molded to his muscular chest and arms. His blue jeans clung to his ass and legs the way they should on a man. His longish blond hair was messy and not in his usual upward style, and his matching scruff was a tad longer than normal.

He pulled me against his hard chest and wrapped his arms around me tightly. "Are you okay?"

Emotions surged inside me, almost uncontrollably. His presence made moisture spring back into my eyes. "No, but I will be." That had been my motto growing up: Suck it up and survive.

"Honey, I'm so sorry." His voice cracked with emotion. "I'll never be able to forgive myself for you getting hurt because of me."

"No, you don't get to do that." I pulled back and stared into his golden eyes. "You did nothing wrong. You can't blame yourself for what that psychopath did. Believe me, if we did, I'd have so much to apologize for." My aunt hated me, and I'd never understood why. After moving in with her following my father's death, she'd completely controlled my mother and me. Even though she and my mother's relationship was unhealthy, my aunt had focused her hatred on me, but I'd rather she hurt me instead of my mother. When I'd told Egan all about my past, he'd listened without judgment. I'd never found someone like him before.

His face softened, and he blew out a breath. "You're right. It's just hard at times."

The sound of crunching gravel under tires and the purr of an engine filled the air as Roxy and Axel were heading our way. They were a few miles out, but with my supernatural ears, I could hear things from a greater distance away.

"Now isn't the time to discuss that." We had so much to do. I stood on my tiptoes and kissed him, enjoying his sweet taste and the feel of his soft lips. After living through this hell of a night, I needed this moment.

The car came into view, breaking the spell we'd fallen under. I glanced over my shoulder as Roxy and Axel got out of the car. Axel's deep-set frown wasn't his normal expression and made him seem intimidating with his buzzed dark hair and piercing brown eyes.

"No sign of her?" That was the only thing that look could mean.

"Not one." Roxy slammed the driver's door shut and pouted. "That's not fucking possible."

"Maybe you couldn't catch up," Egan suggested.

"There's no way in hell." Roxy crossed her arms and marched over to us. "I drove fast enough to catch up."

"She isn't lying." Axel shivered. "I thought we might die. She almost rolled the car trying to catch up to her before we hit the main road."

"Don't start with me." Roxy placed her hand on her hip and glared. "Your crying didn't help matters."

"I was not crying." Axel breathed rapidly. "I was yelling out of fear for our lives."

I'd never seen these two argue before. They were

usually in sync, but stress had a way of bringing out the worst in people. "I'm sure it was the intensity of the moment. It's been a rough night for everyone."

Roxy's shoulders slumped. "You're right. It's been rougher for you than the rest of us. I just feel like a failure for letting her get away."

"Babe, you did everything possible." Axel wrapped an arm around her shoulders. "Believe me when I say that. I was right beside you in that car."

The corners of her mouth tipped upward, and a smile broke free. She wrinkled her nose. "I hate you. Just know that."

"The feeling's mutual." He winked and kissed her forehead. "Let's join the others."

The four of us stepped through the huge hole in the cabin wall. Ollie stood against the wall with Donovan watching his every move as if he might fly away.

"What's the plan?" Roxy asked. "And why is he still alive?"

"Apparently, the witch was controlling him." Lillith shrugged. "Now Jade has the magic bracelet and made him cut himself." She gestured to his wound, still dripping blood.

"You totally should have had him cut his penis off." Roxy faced me. "That would've been a better test."

"Uh, no," Ollie said in a very high-pitched voice. "Please don't." He stared at me with pleading eyes.

He actually thought I would do it. Roxy sure enjoyed messing with people, and keeping a smile off my face took a lot of work. "She has a point."

He placed his hands on his chest. "Please, I'll do anything."

Now he'd made me feel bad, taking all the fun out of it.

"No, I won't do that, even though I should after all the shit you pulled, willingly or not. You could've warned us."

"I couldn't," he whined. "She prevented me from telling anyone."

"Oh, come on," Lillith growled. "You could've written it on a piece of paper or done something to alert us."

I agreed, but lecturing him wouldn't do any good.

Egan tensed beside me, breathing rapidly. "You prick. I don't care if she was controlling you. It's taking every ounce of self-control I have not to pummel you."

"Look, I don't know much, but I want to find her, same as you." Ollie dropped his hands. "My cast can help. The more people searching for her, the faster we'll find her. One thing is certain: if you or Jade go to the thunder, she will track you using Jade's blood."

"Cast?" I asked.

"Yeah, a group of falcons is called a cast, like a wolf has a pack," Ollie answered.

"What? How?" Axel's brows furrowed. "If she has Jade's blood, how can she track Egan?"

"She was hoping his emotional tie to her would help us track him, but she wasn't certain." Ollie pointed at me. "But now they're fated mates, which means they share the same soul, and her blood can be used to track them both."

That sounded logical in a creepy way. *What do you think?* He wasn't lying, so he believed the words, even if they weren't true.

If there is a chance we might lead her to the thunder, we can't risk it, Egan said as he intertwined our fingers. *I can get someone to come here to help us find her.*

That sounded like a decent option. If they came to us, we wouldn't have to worry about leading her to them. *They'll have to be careful. She'll try to put a locator spell on them too, so whoever comes needs to stay until everything has settled.*

You're right. He squeezed my hand lovingly.

"As fun as this is, I want to get the hell out of here." This place would always be linked to my second worst memories of locations now, coming in right after my aunt's house. "Can we head out?"

"Of course." Sadie placed a hand on her heart. "I wouldn't want to be here longer than necessary either. Seeing you like that was horrible enough. But what are we going to do with him?" She nodded at Ollie.

"We'll bring him with us." Egan's tone held an edge. "There's no way we're letting him out of our sights. I'll stay with Jade in case the witch shows back up in their room, and either Axel or Donovan can stay with my roommate. Ollie can take one of their spots in their room."

The thought of Egan staying with me excited me way too much. I hadn't considered how I felt about staying in my dorm room alone after Vera had made it clear she wanted to kill me. "They may not be too thrilled with that." Egan had thrown the plan out there without verifying it with anyone.

"No, it's fine," Donovan agreed. "That's the best plan. We want him close by."

"All right, then." The decision had been made, and I was desperate to leave. "Let's go."

"Wait ... maybe I'm not okay with staying with a wolf shifter that would enjoy killing me." Ollie scoffed. "I don't know them. What if they hurt me?"

"We won't," Donovan spat. "Or are you calling us liars? Can you not smell a lie?"

"Fine." Ollie's shoulders sagged. "It's not like I have a choice. At least, I'll be on campus for my classes."

"He can ride back with us." Egan turned toward his Jeep.

As our group headed outside, a nagging feeling ran down my spine. I stopped in my tracks and spun around to face the woods.

CHAPTER THREE

The creepy feeling of someone watching overwhelmed me. But I scanned the woods and didn't see anything out of the ordinary.

Egan's hand tightened on mine as he linked with me. *Someone's out there.*

Yeah, but I don't see a damn thing. This night kept getting worse and worse. I'd figured it'd been Ollie watching me, but it couldn't have been just him. *Do you think it's Vera?*

No. He released my hand and walked a few steps toward the trees. *She'd be cloaked, so we wouldn't be able to sense her. It's something or someone else.*

The feeling vanished. That was so strange and unnerving. Could she have someone else tracking us? I hadn't considered more people could be involved. I turned to the car and realized everyone was tense. They'd felt it too.

How I wished I was only being paranoid.

"How many others are working for her?" I asked Ollie.

"I ... I don't know." He rubbed his hands together. "She was always alone around me. I thought I was the only one."

Dammit, he wasn't lying. He didn't have any helpful insight.

"Let's go." Egan unlocked the Jeep and waved us on. "Everyone get in. We'll be safer on campus."

That got us all moving.

Lillith, Katherine, Roxy, and Axel ran to the Honda as the rest of us rushed to Egan's Jeep. I climbed into the front passenger seat and felt bad when Sadie slid into the back seat, positioning herself between Ollie and Donovan. Under normal circumstances, I'd sit in back, but after Ollie had held a knife to my neck, I hated the thought of being around him.

I couldn't hold in a chuckle when Axel jumped into the driver's seat. Roxy pouted for a second before giving up and getting in the front passenger seat of the other car. Axel hadn't been kidding when he'd appeared less than thrilled about Roxy's driving. She was the type to act first and think about consequences later.

When the cars moved forward, my breathing hitched, revealing how upset I'd been. Now that I felt safer, my body sagged against the car door. "Shit, I'm getting blood all over the interior."

My shoe wasn't overflowing with blood anymore, but my pant leg was soaked, and blood coated my shoes.

Egan didn't even flinch. "Don't you dare worry about that. I can clean the car or buy a new one. I'm more worried about getting you clean and dry someplace safe."

Donovan chuckled from right behind me. "Besides, it's about time his car had blood spilled in it."

"Is this normal for you all?" I got that Sadie had contended with a man who'd lied about being her father, but I hadn't expected that all of them had experienced so much violence.

"It is, unfortunately." Sadie sighed. "I'd hoped that things would have calmed down, but it's obvious that's not happening."

"You don't have to be part of this." Egan glanced in the rearview mirror at her. "They're after my thunder, for God knows what reason. It doesn't have to affect any of you."

"Are you serious?" she asked, her nostrils flaring as she shot daggers at Egan. "You fought with us when you didn't have to. Did you think we wouldn't return the favor?"

"You still have your own pack to get settled." Egan's hands tightened on the steering wheel. "And you're getting to know your dad."

"Dude, come on." Donovan sounded as upset as Sadie. "There's no way we're not helping you figure this out. Besides, you may not be a wolf, but you and Jade are like pack to us. And wolves take care of their pack mates."

"You guys really are odd." Ollie leaned forward and looked at each one of us. "You do realize most races keep to themselves, but you have vampires, dragons, wolves, and fae all in the mix."

"Things are changing." Sadie arched an eyebrow at him. "More races are coming together. It'll take time, but we must realize that coming together as a community will make us stronger and better than isolating ourselves. When we come together, we can help each other with our resources."

"Or races can hold their resources as leverage over one another's heads." Ollie scoffed. "You saw what that witch did to me. I'm all about sticking to my own kind."

I couldn't blame him there. People survived by keeping their heads low and focusing on themselves. But the way Sadie had described the world she envisioned sounded pretty damn good. Hell, I hadn't been around them long, but if anyone could accomplish that vision, it was this group.

However, if Ollie and Sadie kept going down this road, it would turn into an argument, so I steered the conversation in a more productive direction. "How did the witch get to you?" That was one thing I'd been wondering since hearing his long-winded story. I opened the hand still clutching the bracelet and examined it. It was a gorgeous piece of jewelry and very authentic. The specks of ash were almost fluffy, confirming they had come from a feather.

"She found me here." He tilted his head. "Okay, not here but at Kortright, on the first day of second semester. I was flying in the woods, enjoying the freedom from my cast. My parents are a little intense. They're the oldest and viewed as the leaders of the cast."

I was all too familiar with overbearing adult figures. "They couldn't be that bad since they allowed you to go off to college." Aunt Sarah had been determined to keep me in her sights.

"I didn't have a choice." He sighed. "Family business and all. They're big-time lawyers who have never lost a case. They expect me to follow in their footsteps, so I chose this school since it's several hours away and doesn't get cold like in the north."

"So Vera caught you in the woods?" Egan turned onto the main road, heading back to campus.

"Not exactly." Ollie looked out his window, watching the trees fly by. "I got tired of flying around, so I stopped on a branch to rest and preen. She found me while I was preoccupied, and when my feather fell, she caught it. She must have been tracking me. I didn't realize the problem until I smelled fire. She burnt my feather right then and there and captured enough ash to put in the bracelet."

"Wait ... did you chase me that day?" Had he been in the woods, making me feel so damn threatened?

"Yes, she told me to scare you off." He scratched his nose. "I tried so hard not to, but I didn't have control over myself. I was a passenger inside my own body."

That description sounded horrible and put his experience into perspective. Too tired to hold my head up, I propped my head against the passenger door window and enjoyed the cool glass against my skin.

"How come we never saw you on campus?" Egan hadn't relaxed one bit. He focused on the road ahead, following behind Axel. "You say you're a student there."

"My classes are later in the afternoon." Ollie yawned. "I needed to work the evening shifts to cover my tuition and board since my parents weren't thrilled about me coming here."

Evenings and weekends were the best times for tips. That was one reason I'd requested the weekends when I'd applied at Haynes.

"Do you know anything else about the witch?" Sadie asked. "Even something that seems insignificant could lead us in the right direction?"

"No," he said with defeat. "I've got nothing. She only came around when she wanted me to ..." He cleared his throat. "... hurt someone and commanded me not to tell anyone about her, what she asked of me, and our connection. Other than that, she left me alone."

He'd been a victim just like me, but that didn't change the fact I needed time before I forgave him. Yes, Vera had controlled him, but he'd hurt me and others. Amber's face popped into my mind.

The Jeep descended into silence, and after a few moments, Egan relaxed enough to take my hand. Today felt like it would never end. So much shit had happened, and I was ready to sleep, hoping tomorrow would be better.

We pulled into Kortright's parking lot, and I sat upright in the car. As soon as the cars parked, we all jumped out.

I cringed at my clothes. "Uh ... I need to change. I don't want anyone to see me like this."

Lillith's skin wasn't as white as she approached us. She took a large sip from the cup in her hand. "We can go behind the buildings and up the stairwell."

"That's ideal since I plan on sneaking in too." Egan stood in front of the Jeep. "Let's get you inside. It's before midnight on a Friday night. Most everyone is still out partying."

Donovan walked over to Ollie and grabbed his arm. "We'll get falcon boy settled, and I'll move my stuff into your dorm."

"We'll come help you," Sadie said as Axel and Roxy followed behind Donovan too.

That left Egan, me, and the vampires behind.

"Let's go," Egan said as he took my hand, and our group walked behind the men's dorm to the women's.

Light and darkness might not affect my vision, but as we walked between the buildings and the woods that surrounded the campus, I searched the trees frantically for anything out of sorts. I didn't feel the tickle down my spine of someone watching me, but that didn't mean the witch wasn't near.

Do you sense something?

Egan slowed, following my gaze to the woods. *I don't.*

Thank God. *I just want to get inside and wash all this dry blood off me.*

We rushed up the stairs, and in my room, I almost cried with relief. Vera's side of the room remained untouched.

Her Star Wars poster hung over her neatly made bed. Even her desk still had her college books sitting to one side.

That stupid feeling of being watched swarmed around me again. "I'm so tired of this feeling." Vera had to be doing this. "This is what I felt the other day before Ollie crashed into my window repeatedly."

"She must be using a spell." Egan rushed over to the desk and opened the drawers. "There has to be something here."

Lillith gestured to the ceiling. "She's astral projecting."

I looked up and saw a faint figure hovering in the air that looked like a ghost. The figure flew through the window outside, vanishing from the room.

"What the hell is astral projection?" They needed to remember to treat me like the supernatural newbie that I was.

"A witch can go into a dream-like state and project herself anywhere to watch over." Lillith shook her head and scowled. "It takes an extremely strong witch to do it, but that just confirms what we already know about her."

"This is ridiculous." This woman was stalking me. There was no telling how often she'd watched us. "How can we stop her?" If she could locate me, she could watch me wherever I went.

"Dad taught me a sigil when I was younger in case I ever needed it." Lillith turned around, looking for something. "I need something to write on the wall with."

"Oh, here." Katherine snatched the Sharpie from my desk and tossed it at the other vampire. "That should work."

The thought of messing up the dorm walls put me on edge, but I'd rather pay to have it repainted than let that psycho bitch hover over me. I bit my tongue as Lillith went to work.

On each side of the window, she drew a symbol that looked like an A with the point to the right and a squiggly line underneath. She drew it on the back of the door too. "There. All entry points to the room are covered. As long as nothing happens to the symbol, you'll be protected."

Egan tensed. "We'll change the locks first thing in the morning."

"Now that sounds like a plan." Lillith yawned. "If you two are good, I'll head back to my dorm. The bed is calling my name after all that shit tonight."

"Same," Katherine agreed and hugged me. "I'm so glad you're okay. Tonight terrified us. We thought we might lose you."

This was awkward. I patted her shoulder and hoped my forced smile wasn't scary. "Thank you for being there for me."

"Always."

The vampires left the room, leaving Egan and me alone. I hurried to my closet and grabbed some pajamas to change into along with a towel. I needed a shower pronto.

I faced the door and came to a stop. Egan stood there, holding the door open.

"Uh ..." I wasn't sure what he planned to do. "Are you going somewhere?" Disappointment flared through me. I'd expected him to spend the night with me, but he'd obviously changed his mind.

"I'm going to the shower with you." He motioned toward the bathroom. "There's no way I'm letting you go in there with that witch looking for you."

"But it's the girls'—"

"I don't care," Egan said and placed a hand on the small of my back, took my towel and clothes, and led me into the hallway. "I can't handle you being alone in there. If anyone is in there, I'll wait outside in the hallway."

His concern for me made me fall for him even harder, which surprised me. I hadn't thought that was possible. "Fine."

The bathroom was completely empty, so Egan joined me inside. I was determined to hurry before someone caught us in here. I turned the water on and stripped, laying the clothes on the shower floor so they could soak. Getting the blood out of them would require some elbow grease. I walked out to grab my supplies, and my gaze landed on Egan. His pupils turned to slits as he took in my naked figure.

My breath caught as need surged through me. I'd almost died tonight, and the thought of him between my legs seemed way more important than taking a shower.

He must have felt the same way because he crossed the room and kissed me hard while his arms wrapped around my body.

I opened my mouth, allowing him access inside. His sweet taste made my head spin, and his hands cupped my ass cheeks. We lost sense of time as we devoured each other.

A door swung open, and I froze. Someone was heading in here, and there was nowhere Egan could hide.

CHAPTER FOUR

I took several steps away from Egan like that would improve the situation despite being completely naked. Now he probably looked like a creeper instead.

Roxy's and Sadie's musky scents hit me.

They rounded the corner of the small hallway, and Roxy wore a shit-eating smile. Glancing at Sadie, she gestured at Egan, then me. "See, I told you she'd be naked."

"She was covered in blood." Sadie lifted her right hand. "Of course she'd be naked."

"Oh, you know what I mean." Roxy sniffed loudly. "Arousal is in the air. I thought we might walk in on dangling bits. I was kinda hoping ..."

A low growl escaped me before I could hold the sound in, but my dragon surged forward at the thought of her seeing Egan naked. I'd taken a step toward Roxy when Egan's arm slid around my waist, pulling me to his chest.

His touch calmed me enough for my dragon to recede.

"She's kidding." Sadie smacked her best friend hard on the arm. "You know you can't joke like that about someone's mate, especially when they're newly mated."

"You're right." Roxy's face turned serious for once. "I'm sorry. I'm just giving you a hard time, but now probably isn't the best time since you're still covered in your own crusted blood."

I realized I was standing stark naked in front of all three of them. "On that note." I pulled away from Egan and saw that I'd gotten some flaky blood on his shirt. Trying not to focus on that, I snatched my towel from his hand and wrapped it around my body. "I'm going to go get the blood out of my clothes and off me."

"You really think you can get the blood out of those clothes and shoes?" Sadie's brows furrowed. "With the amount of blood you lost, you probably can't soak them long enough to get them clean."

Unfortunately, I agreed with her, but I was low on money and didn't have a job. I needed to salvage them. "It's worth a shot."

"Look, we can get you another outfit tomorrow." Egan pushed a piece of my hair behind my ear. "There's no point in trying to save them."

He was right even if I didn't have the cash. "Fine." I wouldn't need that outfit since I wasn't working at the steak-house anymore.

"Girls are trickling in." Roxy tapped her ear. "You need to get out of here before someone else catches you."

"You two are staying here with her, right?" Egan tensed, not thrilled about leaving. "That witch astral projected into the room right before we came here."

"Yeah, that's one reason we're here." Sadie winced and shook her head. "We've got to figure out who the hell she is and what we're up against."

"Later," Roxy said as she grabbed Egan's arm, tugging him to the door. "We'll protect her. Go hide in her room."

Egan put my pajamas down on a bench and glanced over his shoulder at me, his face drawn with concern. *If you feel anything odd, let me know. I don't care if I get in trouble for being here. I refuse to let anything happen to you. You've been through enough.*

I promise. After ignoring the danger of going to the steakhouse, alerting him to anything that felt off seemed more than fair. He hid it well, but tonight had taken a toll on him. *Now go.* I headed into the shower, picked up my soaking wet clothes and shoes, and threw them away. Everything inside me screamed to keep them, but I had a feeling I'd have to fight Egan and the girls if I tried.

Needing to get the blood off me, I stepped into the shower, letting the hot spray hit my entire body. No matter how many times I lathered, I still felt like I had blood all over me. I scrubbed myself hard.

Footsteps headed my way, and Roxy called out, "You okay in there? It's been a while."

"Yeah, sorry." I'd lost track of time, but I finally felt somewhat clean. I turned the water off and dried off with my towel. As I stepped back into the tile hallway, I turned left and stopped, noticing my reflection staring back at me in the mirror. My dark hair looked a touch darker when wet, but that was normal. Between the dark circles under my brown eyes and my abnormally pale skin, I looked like death walking. No wonder I didn't feel up to par.

"Are you okay?" Sadie stepped into the view, her eyes lined with worry. "Can I help you with anything?"

She had good intentions, but I hated when people looked at me like I was a charity case. That was the same expression everyone had worn at my dad's funeral, but I had to remind myself that Sadie would never intentionally make me feel that way.

Pushing down my prickly feelings, I inhaled sharply. "Yeah, sorry." They were probably eager to leave the bathroom. "Just out of it." I rushed into the open room with benches that everyone used to blow-dry their hair and put makeup on. I slipped into my pajamas and brushed my hair.

"Hey, I wasn't rushing you." Sadie sat on the bench beside me. "You were just back there a while, so I thought I'd check on you."

I paused from brushing my hair. "No, I know."

"Uh, speak for yourself." Roxy squinted at me with a cocky smirk. "I'm all about rushing her. I don't want the scary dragon to come in here and eat us because he thinks we're messing with his mate."

Even though she was trying to make me smile, I couldn't. "Sorry, I'm not in the best frame of mind."

"You almost died tonight." Sadie sighed and rubbed my arm. "I've been severely injured before, and right when you think you're fine, you reach your breaking point. What you need is a good night's sleep in your mate's arms."

"Maybe something more than sleep." Roxy waggled her brows. "That would definitely put you in a better mood."

The thought was tempting, but I felt way too tired to do more than think about it. Maybe he could help me forget in the morning. I picked up my wet towel and headed to the door. "I'm calling it a night."

The two of them followed me out and walked me to my dorm. Inside, I found Egan already changed and lying on my bed. He had some crackers, Doritos, and two Cokes sat on my desk. When he saw me, he held out his arms for me.

My legs propelled me forward, and I climbed into bed beside him.

Egan nodded at Sadie and Roxy. "Thanks for keeping an eye on her."

"No problemo." Roxy winked at me. "She needs rest, and I need her back to her usual self."

"We all want that." My body grew numb. I laid my head on Egan's chest, listening to the steady heartbeat.

Sadie turned the lights off and closed the door. Within seconds, I drifted into a deep sleep.

THE SUN SHONE between the blinds, hitting my eyelids. My eyes fluttered open, and the last twelve hours flooded back. I searched for Egan, but he was nowhere in the room.

I linked to him, worried something had gone wrong. *Where are you?*

Dammit, I was hoping to get back before you woke up, Egan responded, sounding like his normal self. *I called my dad this morning to inform him of what happened last night. I didn't want to wake you, so I snuck out and got you a cup of coffee. I'm heading up the stairs and will be there in a second.*

Coffee sounded amazing, but the part of him telling his dad did not. The last thing I wanted was for his parents to disapprove of me. If they thought this was happening because of me, they might discourage Egan from being with me.

The door opened, and Egan stepped into the room. His hair was styled in its usual way, and he wore a clean, black, button-down shirt and blue jeans that left very little to the imagination. My body became alert, and I hadn't even taken a sip of coffee yet.

"Good morning." He shut the door, locked it, and put the drink on the desk next to the two Cokes we hadn't touched last night before kissing me quickly. "Are you feeling any better?"

"Mmhmm." I grabbed the back of his neck and pulled him down so his lips met mine again. *But I won't be if you stop doing this.*

Well, we can't have that, he replied as he slipped his tongue into my mouth. *I wouldn't be a good mate if I didn't oblige.*

My eyes stayed locked on him as he removed his shoes and slipped into bed. He pulled me into his arms, but that wasn't nearly close to enough.

Overcome with need, I slipped my hands under his shirt and traced his six-pack with my fingertips. His body shuddered, empowering me.

I sucked in a breath, enjoying the unique mixture of his citrus scent and sweet vanilla taste. He reminded me of happiness, which seemed altogether fitting.

Pulling back, I yanked the edges of his shirt up. *Off. Now.* I needed to feel his skin, and the clothes were an unnecessary barrier.

Maybe we should rest, he suggested and pulled away slightly. *You almost died last night.*

Which is exactly why I want to feel alive. I ripped the buttons from his shirt, slid the flaps open, and ran my hand across his body. *Please don't say no.*

I could never do that. His lips slammed back onto mine, and his desperation bled through the bond. He wanted this as badly as I did. We both needed the connection.

He trailed kisses down my neck, and his calloused hands brushed against my skin. His breathing picked up as his teeth grazed my skin. He wasn't being nearly as gentle with me this time around, and it turned me on even more.

I slipped my shirt off and tossed it on the floor. I hadn't worn a bra to bed, and his eyes landed on my breasts.

You're so fucking gorgeous, he growled and placed his mouth over my nipple. He bit gently and flicked his tongue. My body blazed.

Not missing a beat, he pushed down my pajama pants and touched between my legs. His fingers rubbed the perfect spot, hard and fast. He wasn't building up at a slow pace; he was desperate to please me ... desperate to claim me again.

One of my hands slid into his hair as I unbuttoned and unzipped his jeans with the other. I then shoved my hand inside his boxers and stroked him as he worked on me.

His breath hitched, and he nipped harder on my breast, creating pleasure instead of pain. My dragon roared inside me, but it didn't seem strange. She needed to connect with Egan's dragon the same way I needed to connect with Egan.

We touched and fondled each other, pushing each other closer and closer to the edge. Right when I almost fell off, Egan stopped and stood, pushing down his jeans and boxers and removing my bottoms.

He moved to slide between my legs, but I didn't want that. I pointed to the bed and linked with him. *Lie down. It's my turn.*

Whatever expression he saw, he didn't attempt to argue. Instead, he climbed into the center of the bed and sat against the headboard.

I took him in, enjoying the view of his skin and muscles. He was hard in all the right places, and my body was buzzing and ready.

In a flash, I straddled him, and when I grabbed him to slip inside, he caught my arm.

One second. He cupped my face and kissed me gently

then moved his head to stare deep into my eyes. *I love you, Jade.*

My heart pounded hard, and not from the sexual chemistry between us. *Look, I know I said it last night, but don't feel obligated to say it back.* Besides my parents, I'd never said those words to anyone else.

You think that's why? His pupils turned to slits. *I've loved you since the moment I saw you on campus. You had my heart from that very first day and will have it for all eternity.*

The depth and sincerity of his words stole my breath. I'd always thought that feeling this way for someone would destroy me, but it made me stronger in so many ways. *I loved you then too, but I was too scared to acknowledge it.* All I'd done was stupidly try to run away.

I know. He kissed me and grinned. *But you needed space and time to catch up. When I was growing up, I spent my entire life knowing there was someone perfect out there for me. You didn't have that opportunity. I'd wait for you all over again because this is worth every ounce of hurt.*

My eyes burned with tears, and the need to mate with him was stronger than ever before. This time, when I guided him inside me, he didn't stop me. We looked into each other's eyes as he slowly entered me.

I rocked on top of him as he filled me entirely. I grabbed the cheap headboard for leverage as I moved faster and faster. His mouth found mine as we moved in time with each other. I slammed him inside me over and over as our bodies gave over to the friction.

Egan's feelings crashed into me like a dam breaking. I felt how much he loved me and the pleasure he felt while inside me. If I thought I'd known how much he cared about me, I'd been wrong. He loved me so much it hurt.

Wanting him to know I felt the same way, my dragon guided me into pushing my emotions toward him. Our breathing and pace increased as we fell over the edge, and an orgasm ripped through us and combined into one. The world shook as everything inside me contracted. I'd never felt pleasure like this before.

We stopped moving, locked in our position. I peppered his face with kisses, giving myself over to him completely.

Something burned between us, and I never wanted it to stop.

A loud knock sounded at the door. The scents were unfamiliar. They had almost a brimstone quality to them.

"Shit," he growled. "I wanted to talk to you before they got here."

"Who?" I asked as an uncomfortable expression flitted across his face. What the hell was going on?

CHAPTER FIVE

Another round of knocking pounded against the door. Whoever waited wasn't very patient.

I climbed to my feet and snatched my clothes off the floor. *Who's out there?*

When I called Dad this morning, he said he'd send a couple of dragons to us. Egan followed my lead and dressed quickly. *I wanted to tell you, but they got here quicker than I anticipated.*

A deep, commanding voice asked from the other side of the door, "Are you going to let us in?"

I glanced down at my clothes and cringed. Great, I was going to meet my very first dragon shifters, outside of Egan, in my pajamas. I wished I'd grabbed clothes from the closet instead of the floor.

Egan finished buttoning his jeans, hurried to the door, and opened it to reveal a gorgeous man and woman.

The man stood close to seven feet tall, only an inch shorter than Egan. He had a similar muscular build but, again, a smidgen smaller than my mate. That was where the similarities ended. The guy had hair long enough that he brushed it back from his face, along with a short beard. He tugged at his tight-fitting black shirt, his gray-green eyes narrowing in annoyance.

The girl was a foot shorter than the guy. She shook her head, her long vanilla-blonde hair brushing her shoulders. "Sleeping in, I see." Her long-sleeved, royal blue shirt hugged her athletic frame, emphasizing her cleavage. Her honey eyes scanned me as the corner of her mouth tipped upward like she found something about me amusing.

The way her face lit up when she looked at Egan, though, almost had me spitting with rage.

She rushed into the room and threw her arms around my mate. My dragon roared, but I pushed her down. My hands clenched into fists, and I forcibly held them at my sides. If I let go of an ounce of self-control, I'd grab the hussy by the hair and yank her off my mate.

My blood boiled at the familiarity between the two, but I reminded myself that Egan had given me no reason to doubt his loyalty. That didn't stop me from feeling self-conscious in my baggy, plaid pajamas next to her.

My mind raced to come up with a witty comment to her very rude remark. "Uh ... yeah." My awkwardness, which had started to disappear after I'd bonded with Egan, hit me full force. I hated that someone had the power to make me feel that way again, adding to my already heightened anger.

Egan returned the hug briefly before wrapping an arm around my waist and pulling me against his side. "She had a rough night. Cut her some slack." His tone was neither friendly nor cold.

"Of course." She chuckled awkwardly and waved a hand at me. "I wasn't thinking. Your parents filled me in on what happened to her. Poor girl couldn't even protect herself."

The overwhelming urge to slap the bitch clawed into me. My dragon wanted to put her in her place, but I didn't know how. I had no control over her, and the girl could kick my ass. Her coming here, looking gorgeous, hugging my mate, and insulting me within a minute of meeting me didn't help. Worse, his parents had told her everything.

On the positive side, I'd experienced feelings like these all my life, and even though the emotions were more intense, I'd learned to keep them in check. If I hadn't, I wouldn't have survived this long.

"Remember, she's only been a dragon for a week." Egan frowned and tightened his hold on my waist. "Jade, this is my friend from childhood, Mindy." He kissed my cheek and smiled proudly at me. "And this is my mate, Jade."

The amount of adoration in his eyes calmed my dragon down ... mostly.

"You're Ladon's son," the guy hovering in the doorway interjected. "It's nice to meet you." He bowed his head slightly.

"And you are?" Egan asked, arching a brow. "You're not from our ... home."

The sound of footsteps heading down the hall alerted us that humans were close by. By the way the man had tensed, he clearly wasn't comfortable here.

Based on what I'd learned, dragon shifters kept to their own race. Even though Egan had been around humans for a little over a semester, he still stood out—or he did to me. He was breathtakingly gorgeous and more of a gentleman than Dad. His slight accent drove me wild and added to his mysterious allure.

The two girls walked past my room, but when they spotted the guy standing at my door, they stopped in their tracks. Obviously, he had the same effect on them as Egan.

The new guy didn't affect me like that, but that was because of Egan.

Without acknowledging the girls, the dragon said, "My name is Draco." He shook his head, oblivious to the girls. "But I live close by, and your dad asked me to come."

We needed to shut this conversation down since we had prying ears. If the dragons weren't used to censoring themselves, he could say something outlandish. *Why don't we go into the woods or somewhere discreet to have this conversation?* The dorm room wasn't big enough for three towering dragons and me, and I had a feeling Mindy would jump at the chance to sit next to Egan on my bed. I wasn't sure I had that much self-control.

Yeah, you're right. Egan lifted his chin. "Why don't you two head downstairs? We'll be there in a few minutes."

"You could come down with us while we wait on her." Mindy frowned. "I haven't seen you in a while, so it'd give us time to catch up."

This girl was pushing my buttons. If my dragon hadn't been up in arms, my human side would've been.

"You'll have plenty of time to catch up with us." Egan gestured to the door. "And I want to stay close to Jade. You two head on down."

Her mouth opened like she might say more, but she reconsidered. Her shoulders sagged in defeat as she turned to the door. "Okay. Don't be too long."

The door shut, leaving us alone in the room, and Egan's attention turned to me. His face wrinkled with concern. *Hey, are you okay? Your emotions were all over the place.*

Peachy. I'd meant to keep the sarcasm from my voice, but my disdain bled through. *I almost died last night. I'm still adjusting to my dragon. And now two strange dragons appeared at my front door.* And one of them had a predatory look reserved for Egan. She wanted to devour him and claim him as her own. *How did they know where to find us?*

I planned on telling you before they got here. He placed his forehead against mine. *Then you distracted me, but I still thought we'd have plenty of time before they arrived. Dad sounded concerned, but I didn't realize he was that worried. I told him to look for us here since I refuse to leave your side.*

His words eased some of my anxiety. *Your dad doesn't want you hurt.* And neither did I. I was thankful they'd sent backup. *But Mindy seems to know you very well.* I hated acting this way, but I needed to know. *Did you two date before me?*

What? He lifted his head and stared into my eyes. *God, no. There's been no one other than you—ever. I never had the desire to be with anyone else.*

But the way she talks to you and looks at you ... Ugh, I felt downright stupid, but I had to be honest with him. *It's like she's very familiar with you.*

We grew up together, and our entire thunder is close. He took my hand and rubbed his thumb along my skin. Some of his anxiety and discomfort floated off him and into me. He sucked in a breath. *Before we realized the severity of our situation, our thunder arranged mateships. When she was born, my parents and her family arranged for us to be together. But when the leaders determined that our numbers were getting too low, they agreed I should try to find my mate and reenter the human world to reintegrate into society. We weren't sure if our fated mates were still out there since we'd been in hiding for so long, but we had to try since our race is dying off. Her parents agreed, effectively terminating the agreement right before I attended Kortright last semester.*

That's why she has that look in her eye. All her life, she'd grown up thinking Egan was hers. Great. *Of course, your parents sent her here right after I put you in danger.* Probably to show Egan how I didn't belong in his world. Here I thought we could get through anything, but his parents' attempt to influence our relationship wasn't a good sign.

You think that's why? Egan's eyes glowed bright yellow. *She's here because she helps younger dragons connect with their animal. They thought she could help you get control faster.*

Are you sure about that? I'd learned in our short time together that Egan thought the best of people. That was one of the traits I loved most about him, but I tended to be more cynical. Our conflicting viewpoints were likely a product of our upbringings, though. *Maybe they hope you two will reconnect.*

Baby, no. Egan kissed me gently. *They're ecstatic that I found you. Besides, I'm the reason you got injured last night, not the other way around. The witch wants to find my thunder and wants to use you to accomplish that. They sent Draco here to protect you while I'm in class and to keep watch at night in case the witch shows up. They can't wait to meet you, I promise. I didn't even think about Mindy, or I would've told you sooner, but it seems like a lifetime ago.*

I'm being stupid, aren't I? Maybe my dragon had more influence than I realized. *It's just ...*

Not stupid at all. His eyes turned to slits as he grinned. *It's natural for us to be protective of our mates, and I won't lie.* His lips touched mine, and his tongue slipped inside my mouth. *It's hot. But it's my job to ensure you don't ever feel that way again.*

Getting lost in his kisses was so easy. My hands wrapped around his neck, and I fisted his hair. He groaned and pulled me closer. His hands slipped under my pants and grabbed my ass, and my body warmed again.

In my mind, there is, and will only ever be you. His words were a promise. *You hold my heart captive, and I love that you do.*

All of my anger and jealousy disappeared as I opened myself up to him. Our minds connected, and my breathing increased. We should stop this. If Egan's parents found out we kept them waiting and why, I wouldn't ever be able to meet them. They'd sent us help, so we needed to figure out our next move.

I stepped back, removing my lips from his. "We'd better get down there. I have a feeling Mindy won't wait long before coming back up here."

"That's true." He licked his lips. "But we will continue this again soon. And when I say soon, I mean like within the hour."

"Maybe, if you behave." I winked at him, enjoying our time alone.

"I love you," he said.

A smile spread across my face. "I love you too."

Forcing my attention to my closet, I pulled out some jeans and an eggplant-colored sweater and changed. Right before walking out the door, I put the broken bracelet in my pocket to keep it close. I didn't want Ollie stealing it from us. He seemed honest, but I didn't want to underestimate him.

In the main lobby, we found Mindy pacing in front of the double doors. She scowled at Egan's and my joined hands.

Annoyance flared inside me. That hadn't taken long.

Egan squeezed my hand lovingly. *It may take her a minute to adjust, but you have nothing to worry about.*

I hadn't considered that she'd probably had her entire life planned out with Egan as her mate, and that had changed in the blink of an eye. Maybe I should cut her some slack.

Draco was leaning against the front desk with his arms crossed and pushed off to follow us out the door.

"Where are we going?" Mindy asked as she walked on Egan's other side.

"Let's go to the woods." Egan turned toward the large brick library. "We'll have more privacy there."

Humans stayed away from the woods, especially with all of the recent deaths. The university discouraged anyone from going out there alone and strongly recommended that groups stay away. They wanted to ensure they weren't liable for anything that might happen to their students.

We walked past the building and the picnic benches and entered the tree line. The pathway narrowed, and Egan quickened our pace so that Draco and Mindy fell behind. We walked a mile deeper before stopping. The sound of scurrying animals was the only noise we heard. We were alone.

Egan cut to the chase. "I expected someone from my own thunder to come here."

"I come from a line of strong fighters and served as our king's protector." Draco didn't sound boastful but rather matter-of-fact. "With the attacks and the witch trying to find your thunder, your parents reached out to thunders across America. It seemed fitting that someone from my family would volunteer to help serve and protect."

"You have a king?" Egan hadn't mentioned the hierarchy, a concept that was foreign to me.

"We did until the royalty went into hiding," Mindy interjected, refusing to be left out.

"If you're the best fighter we have, then that's fine,"

Egan said as he looked at me. "All I care about is making sure she isn't placed in harm's way again."

Draco nodded curtly. "My goal is that none of us are. We don't need any of us getting injured or tortured into revealing the location of our thunders. That would cause problems for us all."

A branch broke a few yards away, and our group fell silent. Something was near, and I didn't recognize their scent.

CHAPTER SIX

The four of us stood still as we listened. At least four people were closing in on us, and they had the same musky smell as Sadie and other wolves. They were wolf shifters.

Their scent grew stronger although they made no other sounds. They knew how to stay quiet, which would have eliminated them from being human if their smell hadn't tipped me off.

Stay behind me. Egan stepped in front of me to protect me. *There are only four wolf shifters. If they're aggressive, Draco, Mindy, and I will take them out.*

Of course, I wasn't part of that equation. Needing protection was really pissing me off. I'd always relied on myself; then this whole new world had made me feel like that was impossible. But rushing in would only get me hurt and Egan too as he tried to protect me. *I can help, though.*

I know you can. He spoke slowly, weighing his words. *But you almost died not even twenty-four hours ago, and you and your dragon aren't connected yet. These are wolf shifters, and they won't hesitate to use their animal.*

I took deep, steadying breaths. He wasn't being a dick. In fact, he was right. No matter how strong I was in human form, I wasn't supernaturally strong ... yet. That didn't make it any easier, but I'd get there. *Fine, but if anything happens to you, I can't sit back and do nothing.* Just like he wanted nothing to happen to me, I couldn't watch him get hurt.

We'll be fine. Egan reached behind and touched my arm. *When I fought alongside Sadie and the others, I took out twice as many as they did. This should be easy.*

I bit my tongue, not wanting to distract him, but arrogance like that usually didn't play in your favor. That was one reason I managed to kick the guys' asses in martial arts. They thought they could beat me easily.

Mindy scowled at us but was smart enough to keep her mouth shut.

"Who's there?" Draco called out, his voice low and damn scary. "Show yourself, and I won't hurt you."

"Like hell, we won't." Mindy rolled her eyes and spoke loudly like she wanted all the attention on her. "Unless they brought me cake, I'm gonna kick their asses for just sneaking up on us. They have no clue we have as good of a sense of smell as they do."

I wondered if most dragons were this arrogant and if Egan was the exception. Either way, Mindy's attitude wore on my nerves.

"If I were you, I wouldn't be so cocky," a deep, growly voice said from only a couple feet away, but he remained hidden in the trees. "You don't know what you're up against."

Something in his words didn't sit well with me. He didn't sound surprised that we were aware of his presence. *Something's off.* My gut rarely led me astray, and it was yelling at me to run. But we were past the point of escape, especially if they had something up their sleeve.

"Oh, please." Mindy giggled and looked at Egan. "Can you believe these guys?"

Four men stepped into view. They were shorter than our little thunder, except for me—they were about my height. They all were shirtless with defined muscles. They didn't look nearly as strong as Egan and Draco, but they could hold their own. The one with dark auburn hair had a wolf tattoo on his upper right arm.

Gesturing to the tattoo and lifting a brow, I said before I could clamp my mouth shut, "Is that to remind you you're a wolf?"

The taller of the four bared his teeth, his dark eyes locked on me. "Do you think you're funny?" The wind picked up, blowing through Dickwad's shaggy bluish-black hair.

Okay, maybe I came off as arrogant too. "No, it's just ..."

Egan tensed and cleared his throat. "What do you want?" He lifted his chin. "Weren't you part of Tyler's pack?"

The one who pretended to be Sadie's dad? My inner alarm rang louder.

Yes, Egan said, his voice strained. *They left when the new alpha took his spot.*

"Ah ... you remember." Dickwad wrinkled his nose in disgust. "I remember you too. You killed my brother that night you stormed our pack."

Revenge was very dangerous and made people desperate. They'd go to any lengths necessary to achieve it.

"I only did what I had to do," Egan said with regret. "I didn't enjoy harming anyone."

"I can't say the same for myself." Dickwad smirked, and his eyes darkened. "Hurting you and the girl you're protecting will bring me immense joy."

"You really think you can take on four dragons?" Draco closed some of the distance between us, positioning himself to protect all of us.

Four was a stretch seeing as I couldn't connect with mine.

"Oh, yeah." Dickwad chuckled as he and the auburn-haired man removed their hands from behind their backs, revealing the chained rope they each had balled in their hands. The other two shifters, who looked like twins, bent down and pulled out two tranquilizer guns from the trees they'd stepped from moments ago. The only difference between the two was that one was an inch taller than the other.

They'd obviously come prepared, but they only had two of each item. They hadn't expected to find four of us. Hopefully, that would swing things in our favor, seeing as we didn't have any weapons of our own.

"I'll give you one chance to come forward willingly. We can do this the nice way or the more challenging way." He glanced from Egan to the other two. "Honestly, I'm hoping you choose the challenging way, but I was asked to give you the option."

"You were asked?" That sounded like he wasn't the one calling the shots. This had to be related to the witch.

He ignored my question like I hadn't spoken and released one end of the rope, letting it fall to the ground. I realized it wasn't a rope at all but a fishnet that when held together looked like a garrote.

"You expect a gun and thin rope to work against us?" Mindy flipped her hair over her shoulder. "I mean ..."

"Oh, it'll work all right, but I don't give a damn whether you believe it," Dickwad snarled at her. "You'll soon see what it's capable of." He motioned for the other three men to step closer. "Silence will equate to resistance, so don't think you've got the upper hand."

"Do you really think we'd offer ourselves up to you?" Draco straightened his shoulders, emphasizing the size of his chest. "Don't insult us. Just move on to the action."

He rushed forward and punched the leader in the jaw. Dickwad stumbled back a few steps before stopping. He rubbed his jaw and growled at the dragon warrior.

The other three wolf shifters sprang into action. The taller twin pointed the dart gun at me. Egan charged at him, and his shirt ripped as his dark olive wings sprouted from his back. He spread his wings, shielding me from the guy's view.

I'd expected him to shift into his complete dragon form, but he didn't. He was half-beast, half-man, and it blew my mind. I hadn't known that was possible.

He linked. *Duck.*

Refocusing on the threat, I dropped to the ground. The tranquilizer dart buzzed over my head, narrowly missing me.

Egan sacked the guy, and they tumbled to the forest floor. The auburn-haired guy sprang into action, slipping the fishnet wire around my mate's neck.

Oh, hell no. No one hurt my mate.

I jumped to my feet and ran to Egan's aid. Draco was still fighting Dickwad, and Mindy had vanished, so I was Egan's only hope.

I'd only taken a few steps when the guy with the other tranquilizer pointed the gun at me again. I knew I had to do something before he fired. At this close range, it would be a miracle if he missed.

Time slowed as I watched the shorter twin pull the trigger. I couldn't reach Egan to help him get out of the wire since I couldn't connect with my dragon, making me that much slower than everyone else here.

Something solid slammed into my side, knocking me to the ground. I spun around, ready to attack the assailant, when Draco's face came into view. His jaw was clenched, and he quickly scanned me for injuries.

"I'm fine." I turned to Egan. "But he's not."

The auburn-haired guy tightened the metal fishnet around Egan's throat, and my mate's face turned red.

"Dammit," Draco hissed and stumbled back, his clothes ripping. Navy blue scales covered his body as he grew larger, shifting from man to complete beast. He threw his head back and roared.

Under normal circumstances, this would not be ideal. We weren't that deep in the woods, but our lives hung in the balance.

"Shoot him!" Dickwad yelled as he focused on Draco. "We need to knock him out."

I stumbled to my feet and noticed that the shorter twin who had been aiming at me was transfixed by Draco's full-body shift. His mouth hung open.

This might be my only chance to knock one of them out. I hunkered close to the ground, staying low and quiet. As long as I didn't make any loud noises, maybe he'd stay focused elsewhere.

My hand hit my jeans pocket, and my fingertips brushed against the outline of the bracelet. Shit, I'd forgotten all about it. If it worked, I could get us some reinforcements.

I placed my hand firmly over the bracelet in my pocket. I wasn't sure I could mind link with jewelry, so I spoke very low. "Ollie, we need you here now. Bring the wolves and vampires with you."

"The girl," Dickwad grunted.

The shorter twin with the gun pivoted toward me and fired, but Draco crashed between us, causing the dart to bounce off his scales like he was bulletproof.

"What the—" the guy started, but Draco bit the guy's arm and jerked his head, throwing the wolf shifter several yards away.

I ran behind Draco, intent on getting to Egan. I couldn't let anything happen to him. *I'm coming,* I promised into our bond as I raced toward him.

Mindy hid behind a tree several feet away. She ran away, abandoning us to danger. That seemed fitting since she'd only come here for her own motives. The bitch had arrived here and tried to lay claim to a mated dragon. From what I'd seen of the supernatural world, mates were treasured across all races.

Egan linked, but his voice was weak, even internally. *No, stay back.*

If he thought that would discourage me, it did the opposite. He was fading fast, and I had to get to him. Draco was already fighting off the other two idiots, which hopefully meant I had the advantage against the auburn-haired guy beating up on Egan.

He had Egan in front of him as he leaned back against the tree for leverage. Egan's wings weren't any help against the way the guy had positioned himself behind him.

I had two options. I could either go under Egan's wings or around them. Around would take much longer but would be more effective. But when Egan's eyes rolled back into his head, that made my decision.

I couldn't let him pass out. If he did, the others would have leverage over us.

Trying not to overthink the situation, I pushed my legs as fast as they would go. I couldn't risk freezing and him getting hurt or worse. *Spread your legs.* I hoped he was conscious enough to do it.

Thankfully, his legs moved a few inches apart, but they shook. It wasn't much, but I'd make do. *Lift up as high as you can when I say go.* I said a little prayer, hoping what I was about to do wasn't stupid. I could wind up hurting him really badly instead of the dumbass behind him.

When I was only a few feet away, I yelled, *Go!*

Egan moved upward, barely, and I kicked right between his legs. I dropped down as my foot went forward, angling to hit the auburn-haired guy in the nuts. I didn't give a damn if it was a cheap shot as long as he released Egan.

"Aaagh," the auburn-haired guy groaned as he dropped the rope to cup his family jewels with both hands.

My mate fell to his knees, taking deep breaths as he rubbed the red marks cutting into his skin.

I snatched the net from the ground, ready to return the favor to the douchebag who had hurt my mate. I approached him slowly, wanting him to anticipate the moment.

He tried to stand but fell back to the ground. His face turned red from the pain, and he leaned over as his stomach heaved. Any other time, I would've laughed, but we were still in a huge fight we possibly couldn't win.

I hoped the asshole did puke so I could kick him in it. He deserved to wallow in his own waste for their unjustified attack against us.

Each step I took, he countered by stepping backward, but in his current state, I was much faster. I released one end, letting the wire net dangle from my fingers, careful not to let the thin wire cut into my skin.

"Jade, watch out!" Egan yelled hoarsely.

CHAPTER SEVEN

Heart pumping faster at the panic in Egan's voice, I jerked my head to the right as Dickwad lunged at me. His eyes narrowed. He clutched the end of the net and swung it over his head like a lasso.

Great, I was going up against the Lone Ranger. It was fitting since we were in the small Southern town of Hidden Ridge, Tennessee.

All I wanted or needed was for this thing to be over.

Draco was locked in combat with the twins. The taller one kept pointing the gun at him without pulling the trigger like he was playing chess. He was being more strategic than his shorter counterpart, who had turned his focus on me.

Getting me out of a net would be much easier than trying to protect me while I was knocked out. I dropped to the ground, but the shifter was too damn fast.

"No!" Egan screamed as Dickwad countered my attack. He released one end of the rope so the net spread out around my body.

The wire cut into my skin, and I cried out in pain. It felt like something was flowing through my blood. My skin wasn't burning; rather, it felt like the magic was inside me. But with each jerk, the wire cut deeper, increasing my pain. My breathing turned shallow, and my eyes watered.

A huge cocky grin filled Dickwad's face as he faced Egan. "Your mate's dragon is getting fried as we speak."

No, the wolf shifter was goading my mate to make him reckless. *Don't listen to him. I'm fine.* I held my whimpers in, refusing to give the enemy any more pleasure in my capture and trying to prevent Egan from freaking out. The nasty sulfuric stench of a lie, though, wafted around me.

Are you lying to me? Egan's pupils turned to slits, but the raw skin around his neck hadn't healed. *I can feel your pain through our bond.*

That had to be why the auburn-haired guy had tightened the wire around Egan's neck: not only to cut off his oxygen and leave him impaired but also to inflict a grievous injury that hurt the dragon.

Rage coursed through me, and I welcomed anything that would distract me from my pain.

Egan stood on wobbly legs as he gathered his bearings. He took deep, rapid breaths to speed up his recovery. Even if the wire didn't have a magical effect on us, an injury like that would take more than a few minutes to heal. If he attacked now, he'd only get hurt worse. *You need to recover. Don't do anything hasty.* I tried to make him listen to reason.

There's no way in hell I'm doing nothing. I can't let you stand there in pain. He stumbled toward the leader. "Let her go. Now."

"Or what?" Dickwad chuckled. "You can barely stand."

If Egan wouldn't act rationally, I'd do what I had to do. "Yet you're standing close to me." I tried to anger him. "You're so brave. A real alpha-type leader." Disdain dripped from each word.

"What did you say?" Dickwad turned to me, his nostrils flaring.

I'd hit the nerve I'd been aiming for, but maybe I wasn't behaving super logically either. Egan and I were determined to take the brunt of Dickwad's wrath to protect each other.

A loud *kak* sounded, alerting me that Ollie was on his way. I'd been worried that the bracelet wouldn't work, but this was a testament to the witch's power. At least, her magic was working in our favor.

I yanked on the thin wire net, trying to get out, but I couldn't tell the top from the bottom. It reminded me of the day at the beach when I'd come so close to drowning. Dad and I had been out in the ocean, jumping waves. He'd held my hand as a large wave had crashed against us, and then a riptide sucked me away from him, pulling me into deep waters where I couldn't tell which way was up. My lungs had screamed for air, and even at the young age of eight, I'd known there was no way I would survive.

Then a strong arm had wrapped around my waist and pulled me to the surface. A boy no more than a year older than me had saved me. I often thought back on that time, sometimes with longing. Not only had it been the last day I'd spent with my father alive and a mom who was functional, but I'd also found someone I clicked with. I'd never found that again—until Egan.

His name brought me back to the present, and I watched my mate attempt to shift into his dragon form, but it was like his dragon couldn't surface.

"Wow, I hadn't expected for it to work so well." The asshole chuckled as he leaned back on his heels, watching my mate struggle. The way he took so much pleasure in watching us suffer spoke volumes about the kind of person he was. "It's entertaining to witness the supposedly strongest shifter fail. Maybe that's the real reason you hid all these years. You couldn't hack it living among other supernaturals."

"Or maybe they had to get away from the stupidity of arrogant jerks like you. After all, your breed likes to sniff each other's buttholes to pass the time."

His jaw clenched. "Say it again. I dare you."

Really? He wanted me to say it again. "You like to smell butt—"

The guy dropped the net and charged at me.

Dammit, Jade. Egan tried rushing toward me, but he was moving slower than me, which revealed how beaten he was.

Dickwad punched me in the jaw, and my head snapped back. My entire body sagged to the ground. Pain coursed inside me and down my jaw.

"You stupid bitch!" the guy yelled as he drew his foot back.

Right before his foot could connect with my side, Egan slid in front of me, blocking the blow. As his back touched my front, the net's magic sprung forward, and Egan twitched in pain.

Egan! I yelled through our bond like he couldn't hear me otherwise. I yanked and pulled at the wire. It sliced into my skin as I desperately tried to get free. I tried scooting back so the net wouldn't touch him, but my body refused to budge.

"Look how pathetic the two of you are." Dickwad laughed loudly, pacing in front of us, and pulled a knife from his hip. "When the wire breaks the skin, a spell enters your bloodstream for the next several hours. It weakens your dragon and makes you easy to hurt or ..." His face contorted into a smirk. "... kill." He shrugged like either option was no big deal.

The breeze carried in our wolf shifter friends' scent, giving me a second wind. They were on their way, and we needed all the help we could get. I kept my face a mask of indifference, not wanting to give away that backup was arriving.

Within seconds, his nose wrinkled as he smelled the oncoming threat.

"We've got more arriving!" Dickwad shouted and turned to the taller twin fighting Draco, and then he glanced over at the auburn-haired guy as he climbed to his feet. The shorter twin remained crumpled on the ground several yards away.

Draco roared as he yanked the gun from the shifter's hands then dropped it. He lifted one enormous foot and smashed the gun into pieces.

"No!" the twin yelled.

The warrior dragon squared up to Dickwad, who was only a few feet away from Egan and me.

Dickwad's eyes locked on the center of Egan's chest. Desperation took hold, and he charged at us.

Egan groaned as I felt him tug at the connection flowing between us.

I'm sorry, but I need to shift. He tugged on our bond harder. *He'll kill us before Sadie and the others get here, and with my dragon in such a weakened state, I need to borrow magic from you.*

Take what you need. I would never turn him down if he was doing it to protect himself. *You never have to ask.* I couldn't handle losing him. He meant way too much to me.

He funneled more and more power from me, but his body didn't shift any more than it already had. His wings spread out, shielding me from the leader's view, but he was sputtering.

I glanced below his wing to see what was going on. The guy was way too close for comfort. *Egan! Move!*

The words must have resonated with him because his head jerked upward, and he turned, wrapping his arms and wings around me. He rolled us out of the way just in time.

Dickwad croaked as he swung the knife, but the weapon caught nothing but air, and he stumbled.

Paws pounded the ground as Sadie and the others reached us. A black wolf ran between two trees, heading straight for us. A light-pink-furred wolf, a vibrant red one, and a dark brown wolf ran right behind the black one, who had to be Donovan.

They'd arrived in the nick of time.

Smoke trickled from Draco's nose as he roared. He flapped his wings, rising into the air, and he flew over Egan and me. He used his feet to claw into Dickwad's shoulders and wedge his talons between his shoulder blades.

Donovan ran past us and charged at the auburn-haired guy, who was picking up the second net from the ground.

The shifter lifted the net to catch the wolf, but Donovan jumped, lunging for the guy's neck. Donovan's teeth sank into the shifter's throat, and he ripped it out.

My stomach roiled, and vomit surged up my throat as blood, tissue, and skin flung in every direction.

A sweet scent arrived as Lillith and Katherine joined us.

"Egan, move." Lillith pushed my mate out of the way and searched for the end of the rope. She found it in seconds.

"Be careful." I swallowed the rising bile and turned away from the fight. The wolves and Draco were fighting, and we had the advantage now. The scent of blood didn't help my queasy stomach, so I focused on Egan's and the vampires' scents. "The wire is spelled, and I'm not sure if it's limited to dragons." Lumping myself in that category was still strange. Maybe when I finally shifted, it wouldn't feel so foreign.

"Got it," Lillith said as she worked diligently on the net.

Katherine stood protectively in front of us, keeping an eye on the fighting. "The fight's almost done, so we're in the clear."

Ollie flew down and landed beside me. He pecked at the wire, creating a small hole in the net.

"Holy shit." Lillith stopped and watched him with fascination. "No wonder you could peck through eyes and people's throats."

My stomach convulsed, and there was no holding it back anymore. The vivid images of the guy's throat, Amber's neck, and the poor girl's eyes flashed through my mind, and I lost it.

I turned my head away at the last second, and my stomach emptied all over the ground. Luckily, I didn't have much in it, so it was mostly bile.

Egan turned to me, concern in his eyes. "We need to get her back to the dorm."

I wiped my mouth with the back of my hand, and the wires cut into my lips. The stinging took hold again from the fresh wound.

Ignoring my pain and upset stomach, I noticed that Ollie had already pecked a decent-sized hole through the net. I gently pulled the wire toward me, and Egan shifted beside me, helping me move the wire around my body.

"Be careful," I reminded him even though we were moving methodically.

We both knew what happened when our skin got

nicked. Within minutes, I climbed out of the hole as Sadie and her pack rushed into the tree line.

"Is everything okay?" I scanned the area for another threat, but I didn't hear or smell anything. The taller twin, Dickwad, and the auburn-haired wolf lay dead on the ground.

"They're going to shift back into human form," Katherine explained as she turned to the shifter who'd gotten knocked out first. "These guys are from Tyler's old pack."

"Yeah, I know." Egan sighed and pulled me into his arms. "They left that night right after the fight and before the new alpha had time to step up."

My stomach rolled again, and I closed my eyes. I buried my face into his strong chest and breathed in his unique scent to block out the blood.

"Thank God you came to help." Mindy's high-pitched voice was irritating. "Here, Draco. I rushed to get you your change of clothes when I saw you shift. I figured they would come in handy."

Was that really how she was going to justify hiding and letting the three of us risk our lives? I pulled back as Draco took his clothes and rushed into the woods like Sadie and the others had.

I made a huge mistake by pulling back because I again saw the dead bodies and blood all over the ground. Egan pulled me back into his warm, safe embrace.

"That one's alive," Egan said. "Let's take him farther into the woods and find out everything he knows."

That was when the realization sank in. We were at war, and we didn't know who we were up against. We needed answers, but if I was struggling with what I saw here, I might not be able to stomach what came next.

CHAPTER EIGHT

E gan's arms remained securely wrapped around me, but I needed to pull away to provide the illusion of strength. No one else here was having this issue. I nuzzled my head against his hard pecs. "Being a newbie sucks."

His shoulders shook with laughter. "Should I be offended? You are in my arms."

"God, no." I was so glad my head was still buried. My cheeks burned, and if Lillith saw, she'd make things worse. "It's just the gore surrounding us."

"I wouldn't say 'no issue,'" Katherine said gently. "None of us enjoy looking at it."

"Yeah, but I'm the only one who puked." It served me right for wishing the one guy would puke. Maybe karma was real.

"It's good to see your fated mate is so strong and durable," Mindy said with a chuckle. "Not everyone is programmed to be part of this life."

Oh, hell no.

Anger burned my blood worse than whatever magic coursed through it. I stepped from Egan's protective embrace and stared the bitch down. "Oh, I'm sorry, is running off and hiding the right way?" I'd considered talking to Egan about what Mindy had pulled to see how he thought we should handle her abandoning us, but she'd helped me make that decision all by my lonesome.

"What?" Mindy's laughter turned high-pitched and nervous.

Lillith popped her hip and stared the gorgeous dragon shifter down. "You're sticking with the clueless act? We all saw you hiding over there when we rushed here to fight." Lillith pointed to a section of trees I'd seen her hiding in just minutes ago.

"You do realize the wolves would've found you." Katherine tilted her head, looking unimpressed. "They could smell you, just like the rest of us."

"There's a good reason for it." She crossed her arms, obviously displeased by the vampires calling her out. She stomped and whined, "Who the hell are these people, Egan? They can't just come here and accuse me like this."

"They're Jade's and my friends." Egan wrapped an arm around my waist, but a small, disappointed frown marred his face. "You know, the kind that would risk their lives to protect the people they love."

"Egan, if you had been in real danger—"

"I was, and so was Jade." He lifted his chin, looking down his nose at her. "You're supposed to protect the people in your thunder, and you abandoned us."

"She's not even ..." She took a deep breath and closed her eyes for a second. Then her bottom lip quivered, but there was no remorse on her face or in her voice as she said, "You're right. I'm sorry. You know I'm not trained for battle; I'm more of a teacher. I froze."

"You did a whole lot more than freeze," Roxy said as

Sadie and their mates stepped into the pathway. "You ran. Who the hell are you and the other dragon anyway?"

"The more proper question is: Who are all of you?" Mindy surveyed our friends and fluffed her hair. "Besides, I'm Egan's ... close friend." She gazed at my mate possessively, and my dragon roared.

At least, my dragon and I were on the same page about her.

"Close friend?" Sadie asked slowly. "What does she mean by that?"

"We're from the same thunder." Egan stiffened. *I'm so sorry. I never dreamed she'd act this way.*

It's not your fault. He wasn't responsible for her actions, but I'd be putting her in her place soon.

"Oh, we're more than that." She smiled sweetly at him. "I'm sure he hasn't told you—"

Scratch that. I'd be putting her in her place right now. "When you were born, your parents agreed to an arranged mateship that is now over." I wouldn't let this girl think she had a chance with my mate or that he might be hiding their arrangement from me. "Yeah, he told me." I returned her sweet smile, batting my lashes.

Roxy walked over to stand beside me. Staring straight at the girl, she said with disgust clear in her voice, "I'm betting since she knows all about you and that we were the ones fighting beside them, not hiding, that should put things in perspective. If it isn't obvious that you're a lot less important than you think you are, we'll have to add *stupid* to your ever-growing list of attributes."

The fact I'd found people who had my back, no matter what, dumbfounded me. I would never trade them for anything, even for a group of asshole dragons.

Something unreadable crossed Mindy's face as she

waited for Egan to step in, but he didn't help her. After a few moments, she scratched the back of her neck and waved her hand. "You're right. I'm coming off like a bitch." She licked her bottom lip and smiled brightly. "I'm sorry. I was overwhelmed. I'm glad Egan has found such good friends who have his back."

"Unlike some people here," Lillith said lowly but loud enough for Mindy to hear. She turned her back to the dragon and glanced at us. "Is everyone okay?"

"Yeah." Donovan nodded and took Sadie's hand. "I can't get over that they were from Tyler's pack."

"I don't know why they'd be working with the witch." Sadie shook her head like she was trying to make sense of it. "As far as I know, they have nothing against dragons."

"I wouldn't be so sure." Egan's shoulders sagged. "Apparently, I killed the dark-haired guy's brother, so maybe it was revenge."

"Maybe." Axel shrugged. "But guys like them just want something to fight against. They don't care what as long as it gains them an advantage."

"Aw, my mate is so smart sometimes." Roxy walked over and kissed his lips.

"Sometimes?" Axel arched an eyebrow. "Just sometimes?"

"You're making this awkward for everyone." She grimaced as her hazel eyes lightened with humor.

"Ugh," the shorter twin groaned from a few yards away.

Draco reappeared from the woods, his hair a little wild, adding to his allure. He nodded at our wolf shifter friends and vampires. "I'm glad you came to help. I was getting worried until you came to our assistance." His accent was a tad thicker than Mindy's and Egan's.

"Hey, you were protecting our friends, so we should be

thanking you," Sadie said, her eyes on the twin as he stirred. "Why don't we all catch up and get him situated?"

"Sounds like an excellent idea." Draco marched over to the enemy wolf, picked him up, and threw him over his shoulder like the guy weighed nothing.

Egan linked as he brushed my arm with his hand. *Why don't you head back to the dorm room? I can get Katherine to go back with you.*

Katherine was the only one nice enough not to argue. None of the other girls would willingly walk away, meaning I wouldn't either. Sure, my stomach might not be as strong as theirs, but I'd get there. *No.* I almost said I was fine then remembered he'd smell my lie. I didn't need to give him more ammunition to try to make me leave. *I want to stay here with you. Others may attack.*

Which is more reason for you to go. He kissed my forehead. *Seeing you hurt like that ...*

Remember, you won't be able to shift back into a dragon for a while. I gestured to his wings, now held close to his body. *You aren't at full capacity either. Besides, what if they attack me back at the dorm while you all are preoccupied?* That line of reasoning was difficult for him to argue against.

You're right. He tensed beside me. *You're in danger either way. At least, with you here, I can make sure you're okay.*

I felt bad. I hadn't meant to stress him, but my gut told me to stay next to him where I belonged.

Draco marched off into the woods, without looking to see if we were following. He expected to be obeyed.

"Well, okay then." Roxy snorted and walked deeper into the woods.

I followed close behind, eager to get away from the three dead bodies, and almost ran into Roxy, who'd stopped abruptly. She spun around, wearing a huge smirk on her face, and stared right at someone behind me. "Where do you think you're going?"

As I spun around, my gaze landed on Mindy.

Mindy stilled and huffed. "Uh, with all of you."

"Don't you know that the person who hides has to clean up the mess?" Roxy gestured to the three bodies across the pathway. "We don't need innocent humans passing through here and seeing this. I know you're a dragon and don't understand how this works, but suspicion is *no bueno* for us."

Mindy's mouth dropped. "But ..."

"Great. So glad you agree." Lillith crossed her arms, staring the girl down. "Unless you don't want to be a team player."

"No ..." She straightened her shoulders. "I ..."

"It would be appreciated." Egan took my hand and tugged me toward Draco. "Besides, we all need to be there to talk to the wolf shifter."

"Fine," she growled, unhappy with her assignment.

I glanced up in the trees and found Ollie perched, watching us. "Will you alert us if Mindy is in trouble?" Even if I didn't care about her, I didn't wish death on her. Maybe today would be the wake-up call she needed.

The bird *kakked* back and bobbed his head up and down.

I couldn't complain about anything he'd done so far, but he could be playing along to disarm me. I shouldn't let my guard down and leave the bracelet where he could get to it easily.

As we walked deeper into the woods, Egan told both groups why the dragons were here and caught Draco up on all of the craziness of life the last month or so. Reliving all the deaths and my own near-death experience wasn't fun, but I forced myself to push past it.

We were a few miles farther from campus and in an area humans didn't frequent. I had to give it to this group, they really went out of their way to ensure their existence remained a secret.

Draco dropped the shifter and stood menacingly in front of him. We didn't have anything to tie him with, so the guys formed a circle around him, making sure there was no way he could get away.

The girls surrounded the guys, so if he escaped the first wall, he'd have to get through us next. We couldn't afford him getting away until we got information out of him.

Stay close to me. Egan linked as he stepped back, his back brushing against my chest. *And warn me if you sense something strange.*

"Hey." Draco slapped the twin in the face. "Wake up."

"Dad?" The shifter groaned, his eyes fluttering open. After a second, he stiffened and sat up straight. He turned his head one way then the other, taking in our group of nine. "Where the hell am I?" No one answered, and his expression changed from one of confusion to immense pain. "Where's my brother?" he yelled.

I hadn't expected to enjoy this interrogation, but watching him realize his brother was dead tugged at my heartstrings. I understood each emotion that flashed across his face because I'd lived through the same thing when I'd found out my dad had died. That day, I hadn't just lost him but my mom too.

"You attacked us," Draco rasped. "Did you expect us not to protect ourselves?"

"No." He shook his head hard. "This can't be real. We were told this would be easy."

"Someone lied." Egan leaned toward him. "And left out important pieces of information."

"We watched the other dorm and knew the wolves weren't out." He chewed on his bottom lip. "We thought it'd be just you and her. We were told to attack before more dragons arrived."

"You obviously underestimated how long it would take them to arrive." Sadie stepped between Donovan and Axel. "Why are you after them?"

"Do you think I'd tell you?" he spat and snarled. "You killed my entire family."

"If your family had been on the right side, they'd be alive." Sadie's light blue eyes glowed. "You sided with a man who killed anything that got between him and what he thought he was entitled to rule."

"Who decides which side is wrong and right?" The twin's face turned pink. "You?" He laughed hard. "And you think you're better than Tyler?"

The gravity of the situation hit me—this was Sadie's fight, and everyone was letting her take the lead. This person was tied to the pack she'd been raised in. This guy hated us because of our alliance with her.

"I never claimed to be better." She kept her gaze locked on him, the alpha wolf inside her rising. "But I'm not a dictator who hurts others. No person should rule over the entire supernatural race. No one can make the best decisions for all. You have to see that?"

"Maybe." The guy lifted his chin defiantly. "But I don't give a shit," he spat. "I'll always side with those who want to hurt you and anyone close to you. I only want to pay the same respect you did to me and my family."

My worst fears were confirmed. This wouldn't be easy.

He wouldn't spill his guts and plead for us to spare him. He would fight us tooth and nail.

Sadie lifted a hand, a pink glow filling her palm.

Knowing what came next, I closed my eyes instinctively.

CHAPTER NINE

I'd expected the twin to yell or cry, so when I only heard animals scurrying around, I was caught off guard. The twin should have been screaming for his life.

I opened my eyes slowly, afraid of what I might find.

Sadie stood in the same pose. The breeze ruffled her rose-gold hair, and her fae magic pooled on her palm. Her magic was the same color as her hair, which made sense now that I thought about it. I usually thought of her as just a wolf, but with her fae half in action, she was mesmerizing.

"Go ahead," the twin sneered. "Hurt me."

Maybe she was building up his anticipation. *Why is she waiting?* I'd rather get this over with than draw it out. I hated the thought of torturing someone, but maybe this was how things worked in their world.

She's at war with herself. Egan reached behind him and brushed his fingers along my arm. *She doesn't like the thought of hurting someone.*

"Do it," the twin screamed, as if desperate for the pain. "Hurt me."

I understood his plea. He'd lost his twin brother. Physical pain would numb the emotional toil tormenting him.

"No." Sadie lowered her hand and inhaled sharply. "I won't do it."

"We need answers," Draco said, his brows furrowed. "If you won't, I will."

"I understand, but if we want to be different from our enemies, we must act differently." Sadie bit her bottom lip and looked at her mate.

Donovan placed a hand on her shoulder and said, "If my mate doesn't think this is right, it's not."

My respect for her increased. She'd made a hard call. "Even if we tortured him, he might not tell us anything." I had a feeling he'd rather die and join the rest of his family in Hell than help us.

"Besides, it's not like we can let him go or hold him captive." We were at a university and couldn't keep taking hostages. Someone would get suspicious. We were already reassigning rooms because of Ollie.

"You're right." Egan pursed his lips. "And we're too much at risk already by staying here. Vera and the others aren't slowing down their attacks, despite humans being around."

"Unfortunately, going back to our thunder isn't an option either." Draco rubbed his hands together. "Not while they can track you two."

I felt horrible since my blood was causing the issue.

Guilt is wafting off you like a broken dam. Egan angled toward me. *There's no reason for you to feel guilty.*

That was what people said to loved ones even when they were to blame. I hadn't chosen to feel guilty, but I couldn't hide the truth. "I'm sorry I've made this whole situation worse."

"You have not." Katherine shook her head. "If anything, you got dragged into this because of us."

None of them looked at me with resentment, which shocked me. They should have been angry at me like I was at myself.

Sadie pressed her lips together. "This would still be happening if you weren't in the picture. The witch would've found another way. You are not responsible."

"Aw, how touching." The twin's mouth twisted into a nasty grin. "Even if they're right, it doesn't matter. You're mated to the only dragon anyone knows about, and between the group that's desperate to find the thunders and the ones who joined them because of what you did to our true alpha and our families, you're all going to die. Every single one of you. And I hope you suffer until your dying breath." He laughed maniacally.

A chill racked my body. This wasn't normal. People shouldn't cherish the thought of others dying, especially tragically. The more I learned about these people who were loyal to a sadistic leader, the clearer it became that they were monsters in every sense of the word.

"You're right. We can't stay here. We could always go back home." Lillith rubbed her hands together. "We'll be out of the way there."

"No, they'll find Mom's pack and your nest. We can't have that. We have to protect them too." Sadie glanced at her pack members as they mind linked together.

I'd learned that wolves could mind link with their entire pack, whereas dragons could only link with their fated mates. Egan had explained that for each strength a race had, it came with a weakness. They believed that because dragons were stronger, they couldn't connect with the entire thunder. Whereas wolves might be weaker, but connecting with their pack gave them an edge. Nature had found a way to balance the races and put them on equal footing.

"We go back to our home." Donovan nodded as the four of them had come to an agreement. "Everyone already knows where we live, and we have a decent-sized pack that will protect us when they do come to hunt us down."

Having a pack helping us sounded amazing, but that also meant more people could get hurt. How many deaths would I have to witness over the next weeks, months, or even years? I had a feeling I didn't want to know the answer.

"What about the humans?" Hopefully, there weren't too many close by. The thought of innocent people, who knew nothing about our war, getting pulled into the conflict seemed unjustly cruel. It was one thing to know what you were up against, but to be clueless ... that didn't seem right.

"Most packs live out in supernatural suburbs," Roxy informed. "There aren't any humans within miles of our pack neighborhood."

Egan faced them. "Are you sure? That would put your entire pack in danger."

"Egan," Sadie said gently, "you, Jade, Lillith, and Katherine are part of our pack as much as any of those wolf shifters. The vampires and you fought right beside us. It'll be nice to return the favor."

"Nice?" Axel wrinkled his nose. "I wouldn't use that word, but everyone is coming. We protect our own."

For me to be lumped in as part of their family broke the last remaining walls that had been partially standing inside. These people had torn down every self-defense mechanism I'd put in place over the years in less than two months.

"What are you going to do with me?" The twin rubbed the back of his neck. "Kill me?" His words sounded hopeful.

I'd been there once or twice. I wasn't sure if I'd been too

much of a coward or too strong to kill myself. Maybe somewhere between the two. But if I'd thought someone had been willing to kill me, I would've begged them to do it in an instant.

Sadie smirked. "Worse. You're coming with us."

"What?" His mouth dropped. "You've got to be kidding me."

"Does that look like the face of someone who's joking?" Roxy asked, reaching around Sadie and waving her hand in front of her face. "I can't see it, but I'm sure it's her normal 'I mean business' face. You know, the one where her mouth is set and her eyes are narrowed as she stares you down."

I looked at Sadie's face and had to say Roxy had the description locked tight. "Yeah, that's the face."

"See." Roxy patted herself on the chest. "I know my bestie's signature look."

"I'm hoping I am welcomed to tag along too?" Draco crossed his arms, making his chest look mammoth. "I need to stay close to those two. I promised Egan's dad."

"Of course." Donovan gestured to the twin. "You protected Egan and Jade, so you're officially welcome."

"Good." He nodded. "If we're going to get going, we better move before it gets much later. The fewer people who see, the better."

"There's a spot through the woods we can pick you up at so we don't have to worry about students seeing him at the university." Lillith pointed northwest. "It's the same place we used when we escaped from the university last semester."

Axel frowned. "How come I don't remember that?"

"Because you and Donovan were almost drained by a vampire, and Sadie and I bit you, saving your lives." Roxy lifted a brow. "You weren't very coherent."

"I hate to bring this up, but Ollie and Mindy need to go too." Egan glanced at me from the corner of his eye.

The fact he wanted her to come with us irritated the hell out of me. "Why? She didn't even help us fight."

"She's right," Lillith said. "We wouldn't be missing much by leaving her behind."

"Dad sent her to help Jade connect with her dragon." Egan lifted a hand in surrender. "It's not that I want her with us, but if she can help Jade embrace her dragon like she does with the younger dragons in surrounding thunders, she'd be an asset."

"I'll keep an eye on her," Draco reassured the others. "I'll make sure she doesn't pull something like that again."

"Then we better get going." Sadie looked at Draco. "Do you need to get your car?"

"No, we flew here." Draco grabbed the wolf shifter's arms. "We'll need a ride or directions to your place."

"We have a van," Katherine offered. "You can ride with us."

Lillith pointed at Draco and the twin. "Why don't you take these two, along with Ollie and Dragon Girl, over to the pickup location, and I'll bring the van over."

"Sounds like a plan." Katherine took off back toward Mindy and the falcon with Draco following right behind, dragging the twin along.

"Please, just kill me," the twin begged as he tried to plant his feet. "I might as well be dead. She'll try even harder to find you with me in tow."

"She?" Draco arched an eyebrow. "Who is she?"

The twin smirked and shrugged.

He was baiting us.

Lilith waved him off. "He's trying to distract us, which

means he's stalling. We need to get out of these woods. He probably means the witch anyway."

"You're right. And either way, *she* will attack us," Draco growled as he spun around, throwing the shifter over his shoulder. "And good, the more people she sends our way, the more information we can get from them and see what kind of numbers we're up against."

"No!" the guy screamed and hit the dragon's back futilely. "Stop."

Come on. Egan touched my arm as we made our way to one of the school buildings. *Let's get our stuff and get out of here.*

I noticed that he was leading me away from the dead bodies, but I didn't put up a fight. I'd seen enough death to last a lifetime and watching Draco kill the twin was something I'd rather not witness. Instead, I followed behind, enjoying the touch of his skin.

I WAS PACKED and sitting on the edge of my bed in the dorm room, waiting on the others to gather everything they needed. I'd packed up my entire life in less than ten minutes. It should have bothered me, but in these types of situations, it was ideal. Except it would've been nice to have had something to preoccupy me longer. Sadie's aunt, Naida, stood in the center of the room, going through all of the witch's items.

"Where have you been?" I hadn't spent much time with her, and she hadn't been a huge fan of mine at the beginning. Ever since Egan and I had cemented our bond, she'd vanished. According to Egan, that wasn't very strange for her.

Apparently, she and Sadie had stumbled across each other last semester at Kortright. That seemed to happen a lot at this university.

"My kingdom is having issues with my eldest brother coming back." She pushed her teal hair over her shoulder, and her matching eyes found me. Her hair contrasted against her golden-pink skin, and her white shirt emphasized her beauty.

"Sadie's dad?" If memory served me right, Tyler had hidden him for over eighteen years in a basement or hidden room.

"Yes." She took a few steps closer to me.

She was the same height as me when I was sitting. I hadn't realized how petite she was until now. "From what I've heard, I thought your people loved him."

"They did and do," she said as she sat at Vera's desk. She opened the drawers and dug inside.

Wow, getting information from her was difficult, but sitting with her in silence was more uncomfortable. "What's the problem?" I hated when people created small talk, but in all fairness, I wanted to get to know her better.

She huffed and paused her snooping. "My younger brother was sworn in as king since we all believed Rook was dead. But, by fae rules, Rook was destined to ascend the throne."

That could be problematic. "Does Rook want it?"

"No, he never did. But fae are sticklers for rules." Naida shrugged, appearing almost human.

I probably wasn't helping, but I hated the look on her face. "It sounds like you dodged a bullet and that fate intervened by allowing your other brother to take the crown."

She glanced at the ceiling and rubbed her chin. "I

hadn't thought of it like that, but you could be right. Maybe you are meant for this world after all."

That was a huge compliment coming from her. Maybe she was warming up to me. Maybe.

Egan's voice popped inside my head. *I'm on my way to get your things. Everyone else is loading up the cars.*

I can meet you out there. I didn't want him to think he had to carry my stuff too. I loved that he was thoughtful, but I didn't want to become a nuisance.

No, please. Not after what we just went through, he begged.

He'd shifted back to fully human not that long ago. I couldn't fault him for being nervous.

"I take it he's on the way?" Naida asked.

"Yeah, how did you know?"

"You broke out into a huge smile. Sadie does that too." Naida shut the drawer and stood. "I am glad that Egan found you. He's a good guy and needs someone beside him for what comes next."

That sounded ominous. "What do you mean?"

The door opened, and Egan stepped inside, he focused on the one bag next to me. His brows furrowed. "Is that all?"

"Yup." One reason why I stressed when outfits got ruined. "Naida, are you packed up too?"

"I don't have much here either." She headed to the door, passing my mate. "I don't need to ride with you all. Let me settle some things, and I'll meet you there."

"Sounds like a plan." Egan placed the strap of my bag over his shoulder. "Call us if you need anything."

She walked out the door, and I glared at my mate. "They could hurt her too."

"Yes, but she can teleport, so she's not at any risk. Plus, she just came back from the Fae Realm, so her powers will be fully charged," he explained. "Now, let's go. The vampires, Ollie, and Mindy are en route. Draco and Sadie's pack are waiting for us at the vehicles."

"Mindy didn't demand to ride with us?" I figured that girl would've refused to leave Egan's side.

"She didn't have much of a choice."

We left the dorm and headed toward Egan's car. I almost asked about my car, but it had been acting up, and I didn't want to risk it breaking down on the road. I already knew how the conversation would play out.

Something cold brushed against my arm. I jerked to the side, looking for whatever it was.

CHAPTER TEN

The chill sank into my bones, but no one was beside me. I stopped in my tracks.

What's wrong? Egan stopped and scanned our surroundings.

I ... I don't know. It still felt like something was hovering over me. The icy coldness wasn't overwhelming like before as I felt a chill on only one side.

Maybe it was my imagination, so I walked a few steps forward, and the chill faded away until it rushed to catch back up. *There's something cold beside me, but I can't see anything.*

He pulled me to his other side and hissed, *That witch is projecting again. There's a faint outline that's harder to see in the sunlight.*

The day just kept getting better and better. But if she could track us and we weren't protected by the sigil, it made sense that she'd be here. For all we knew, she'd watched the entire fight in the woods. "Let's go." Standing here with her hovering over us did not sound appealing in the least, and in a car, we'd be constantly moving.

"We need to move. The witch is here, watching us again." Egan informed the others as he pulled his keys from his pocket and hurried to his Jeep.

"No time like the present," Roxy said and climbed into the backseat of the Honda, next to her mate.

Donovan got behind the wheel with Sadie sitting in the front next to him.

Rushing to Egan's Jeep, I planned on sitting in the back passenger seat since Draco was so large, but he beat me to the punch, leaving the front passenger seat open. I wasn't in the mood to argue since I wanted to get the hell out of there.

As I slipped into the car, the chill of the witch overcame me again.

She had to be trying to antagonize me. Following my gut, I smacked the cold spot next to me and watched the hovering figure dissipate. I smiled, but my victory was short-lived.

The apparition reappeared beside me.

Here I thought I'd figured out something on my own. I should've known better.

Egan slammed the driver's side door closed, put the key in the ignition, and spun out of the parking spot, leaving the witch behind.

I'd expected her to catch up to us, but warmth returned. "That's weird. She's gone."

The warrior dragon threw his legs on the bench and lay back against the car door. "She doesn't want to spread her magic too thin and will wait until later to come looking for us."

"It's wise that we're heading to Donovan and Sadie's pack instead of Titan's or Cassius's mansion." Egan caught up to Donovan, and his body relaxed a little.

"Who are they?" Sometimes, they forgot I didn't know all the players involved.

"Titan is Sadie's mom's mate." Egan paused, grinning. "I've never said it quite like that before, and it's kind of a mouthful."

"You do realize a human would've said stepdad, right?" I teased.

"True, but there aren't any humans in the car." He winked. *Not after we claimed each other.*

My body warmed at the meaning behind his words. Images of his naked body flashed into my mind, and I squirmed uncomfortably in my seat. It would have been nice if Draco hadn't been in the car.

Draco cleared his throat loudly in the backseat, letting me know he could smell my arousal.

For the first time, being a witch didn't sound so unappealing. Maybe I could turn invisible and never have to face Draco again. I wasn't sure if I could come back from that with him.

Egan's shoulders shook with laughter. *Don't be embarrassed.* He took my hand, leaving one hand on the steering wheel. *All mated shifters get like that. In fact, I can't wait until I get you alone again. After seeing you hurt, confirming our mate bond again would bring me comfort.*

From what you've all said, it only takes one time to complete the bond. If he was going to make light of my embarrassment, I'd give him hell another way. *So if that's the only reason you want to do that, you don't need to feel pressured or worried.*

You know that's not why I want to do it. His golden eyes lightened, and his pupils turned to slits as his dragon peeked through. *I just love—*

"How long have you two been mated?" Draco asked

loudly to get our attention on him and off each other. Now Egan smelled spicy with his sexually charged thoughts. Was that better or worse for me?

"About a week." Egan squeezed my hand as his focus returned to the road ahead.

"So, very new." Draco yawned.

"Are you okay," I asked, directing the conversation away from Egan and me. "You sound awfully tired."

"Between the fight and flying to meet you early this morning while the night sky hid Mindy and me, it's already been a long day. I had to leave my thunder, meet Mindy a few miles away from your thunder, then fly the rest of the way here."

"My parents and I appreciate you coming here." Egan glanced in the rearview mirror at him. "We have over two hours left on the road if you want to take a nap."

"Yeah, I may take you up on it. Once we get there, I'll have to get familiar with the area. I'll keep watch on the first night."

He made it clear that his priority was to protect us. Egan's parents had picked a good one to send our way. *He seems sincere.*

It's interesting that my parents sent someone from another thunder, though. A small group of representatives get together a few nights every year at a secret location only they know about, but other than that, I didn't think they talked to each other much.

You have a way to communicate with each other, though, right? In case a thunder is attacked or the king is in danger? They had to have a plan in case something went horribly wrong.

Egan placed his hand on my thigh. *Yeah, they have a cell*

phone they keep for emergencies. I just didn't expect them to use it.

With the witch looking for an entire thunder, if not all of them, the entire race is at risk. Do you have any idea why someone wants to find you all?

We were forced into hiding because we were being killed off by the Fae Dragon King. Egan frowned, and the knuckles around the steering wheel turned white. *Dragons are originally from Fae. Hell, some dragons still live there. Dragons are viewed as the strongest race, and a group of people thought that by controlling us, they could control all the races.*

It always came down to power. *If dragons are originally from Fae, why are you on Earth?* Not that I'm complaining. The thought of never meeting Egan broke my heart.

Honestly, the story is a little gray since we've been here for centuries, but it had something to do with the youngest brother claiming he should be king because the eldest brother wasn't fit to rule. The details are unclear, but the older brother left Fae to give his brother the crown, and many dragons followed him to Earth.

I was missing an important piece of the story. *Why would them coming to Earth negate the claim?*

Because Fae creatures lose their magic the longer they're here on Earth. The eldest brother sacrificed his power to get out of his brother's way.

But dragons are powerful. That had to have pissed the younger brother off. *You guys don't seem low on power.*

From what my father told me, we've evolved over time to become as strong as we were in Fae. At first, when we settled here permanently, we were really weak. After only a few decades, our magic adapted, mostly because our fated mates were human, binding our magic here instead of Fae.

I placed my hand on top of his. *How is that possible? You would've had fated mates back in Fae too, right?* The thought of him having another potential match didn't sit well with me.

In Fae, we didn't have fated mates like here, and a dragon can easily live for thousands of years. In a way, finding out we had fated mates confirmed we were meant to be in this world.

All of that information was a lot to take in at once. That was one thing I'd learned about the supernatural world. It was large, fast-moving, and there were so many things at play my head was constantly spinning. As a human, life had been simpler. All I'd needed to do was focus on surviving and staying invisible. Being invisible wasn't really an option now.

One question had been tugging at the back of my mind. *Mindy mentioned your king may be dead. Is that true?*

None of us know. The royal family went into hiding to prevent other races from trying to gain leverage of us and control our kind. Only a few knew the location. Over time, we all lost track, so the rumor is they're dead, but it hasn't been confirmed. I think the royal family is out there somewhere.

It was tragic that they'd had to hide away their royal family. *So your people were attacked and hid?*

Egan's eyes narrowed to slits. *Yes. You see, we left Fae because of politics. The last thing we wanted was to get involved with it here. The dragons that were captured were killed because they refused to work for the Fae Dragon King and couldn't tell them where our king was. Eventually, the fae dragons started kidnapping people they thought could be dragon mates to use them as leverage.*

What? They kidnapped innocent humans. *How do they determine who's a potential mate?*

Egan sighed. *If they thought a dragon looked too long at someone or seemed overly interested. Really, it was guesswork, and many people got hurt out of desperation. That's when we decided to close ourselves off and hide until our population dwindled to alarming numbers.*

You were successful on all accounts, then. Despite all of the shit we'd been through, I wouldn't change us meeting. I'd never felt so happy, even when my dad was alive. I leaned over and kissed Egan's cheek. *I'm glad you got to be the test case. I don't know what I'd do if I never found you.*

He turned and kissed me quickly. *I always felt a tug to leave the thunder. Now I know it was you. I would've found a way to leave. Your pull was too strong.*

A low snore sounded from the backseat, ruining the moment. We chuckled, and I leaned back in my seat. The rest of the ride passed in amicable silence.

DONOVAN PULLED off from the interstate right outside of Nashville. I didn't know why, but I hadn't expected them to live near a bustling city. However, we were on the outskirts, so the idea wasn't unfathomable.

I kept anticipating the cold brush warning me of the witch's return, but I'd only felt Egan's comforting presence the entire ride. I enjoyed the reprieve but knew she'd make her presence known eventually.

We pulled onto a gravel road far from civilization, which wasn't surprising since most packs wanted to stay off the humans' radar. We drove through the woods, and a few miles in, a quaint neighborhood came into view.

The dwellings looked like standard middle-income homes with the typical vinyl siding and a uniform feel of grays, yellows, and blues.

Draco leaned forward between the front seats. "This is their pack home?"

"Yeah." Egan pulled onto a paved road and followed Donovan through the subdivision.

People were out in their yards, waving to the shifters as they drove by. A few children even chased after their cars, thrilled to see the four of them.

I chuckled. "They're like celebrities."

"It's a fair assessment." Egan waved at a few people. "Donovan and Sadie are the pack alpha and alpha mate, with Axel and Roxy as the beta and beta mate. Tyler drove this whole pack into the ground, and they were the ones who saved them."

The pack probably viewed them as their saviors. That was a lot more amazing than being an actual celebrity.

We pulled up to two corner-lot houses across from each other, surrounded by trees, at the end of the road. Lillith's van sat in the driveway of the sky-blue house beside the one Donovan pulled into. She, Katherine, and Ollie stood outside near the woods, searching for something in the trees, their bodies rigid. Lilith rushed over to us.

I threw open the car door, and Egan was beside me in a flash.

Something had to be very wrong. Then I realized Mindy was nowhere to be found. "Where's Mindy? Is everything okay?"

Lillith glared at Egan and growled, "We have a fucking problem here."

CHAPTER ELEVEN

S adie and the others hurried over to us.

Roxy asked, "I'm assuming the problem centers around a certain blonde dragon shifter who is missing and has already caused a lot of drama?"

Katherine grimaced. "The very one."

"What did she do?" Egan asked,

I understand why Dad sent her, but I wish he would've sent someone less skilled. If she's just going to cause problems, it'd be better if she wasn't around.

From the first moment I'd seen Egan, I could tell he was smart, but I'd been worried he'd been blinded by Mindy's antics. That statement, though, eased my concern. *It's not your fault. You didn't make the call, and I'm sure your father had no clue either.*

"This shouldn't surprise you, but she hasn't made the best first impression, so I was keeping an eye on her." Lillith's nostrils flared. "I asked her to help carry our stuff into the house. Well, about five minutes ago, I started looking for her, and we can't find her anywhere. There's no telling how long she's been gone."

"Where would she run off to?" Sadie's brows furrowed. "She doesn't know anyone here."

"I know, and the entire way here, she made it clear she wasn't thrilled about staying with a wolf pack." Lillith sighed. "I thought she would help with unpacking. I mean, that's not scary or threatening. She must have left while we were preoccupied, but I'm a little worried about how she disappeared. Do you think she went back to the thunder?"

Even though I would love for her ass to be gone, the witch could track Mindy back to the thunder. "Surely she wouldn't." If Egan's family got hurt, I'd feel responsible.

Ollie put his hands in his jeans pockets. "Maybe she's walking around the neighborhood. We were just jammed inside a van for a couple of hours."

Axel shook his head. "We didn't pass her on the way in. She's gone or out in the woods."

"Let's see if we can find her." Maybe she wanted to get away for a few minutes. I wouldn't blame her if she did, but she should've given them a heads-up.

"Do you want me to take to the sky?" Ollie gestured to the house. "I can shift and help search for her."

"That'd be great." Donovan took off toward the light blue house Lillith's van was parked in front of. He sniffed and waved for us to follow. "Come on, it smells like she headed into the woods."

At least, her scent was still on the ground. Maybe that meant she was close by.

We followed after him, and her cinnamon-brimstone smell surrounded me. Even though my senses had improved after Egan and I had completed our bond, they kept getting stronger and stronger the more I used them. I was glad they were improving gradually because they'd overwhelmed me at first.

Sadie caught up with her mate, and they took the lead. Even though dragons had an excellent sense of smell, the wolves had the clear advantage, so it was smart for them to go first.

Wings flapped overhead as Ollie caught up to us high in the sky.

Hopefully, one day, I could fly like that, even if only at night, hidden by the darkness.

Are you okay? I asked Egan. It rubbed me the wrong way that I felt inclined to ask him that, but I had to remember they were childhood friends.

He intertwined our fingers, and annoyance flowed through our bond. *Yeah, I'm fine. She pulled stuff like this all the time growing up. Back in the day, she liked sneaking away and testing boundaries from time to time. Hordes of people out looking for her made her day.*

That didn't surprise me. She was still territorial over Egan despite our bond, which fit that description. *You aren't worried?*

Not really. Egan shrugged. *But she should've told Lillith and the others instead of running off like that. I don't blame them for worrying.*

The woods grew thicker, and a few squirrels ran by, oblivious to us. The animals were acting normal, suggesting nothing horrible had happened. Granted, even when the wolves had attacked us, the animals had acted the same way, so maybe that wasn't the best indicator.

The thickening trees gave ample shade from the sun high in the sky. I could see why the pack had picked this area to live in. It would be a nice place to run and hunt in their animal form. Though it was February, warmth surrounded us, making this feel more like a hike instead of a search party.

Sadie turned left, keeping close on the scent. "It smells like we're getting close."

After a few steps, a loud cry sounded as if someone were in pain. Panic pulsed through me. It sounded like Mindy.

Without thinking twice, I took off heading in that direction. I ran so fast I caught up with Sadie and Donovan.

"Jade!" Draco yelled after me. "Stay behind me."

If he thought I would stop and wait for him, he'd learn otherwise. Even if I didn't like the girl, I didn't wish her harm.

The trees parted, revealing a large clearing with Mindy standing in the center. Her back faced us, and her shoulders heaved. Her shirt was ripped at her right shoulder, exposing a deep wound as if someone had stabbed her. Blood oozed from the wound and trickled down her arm.

Egan pushed between Sadie and Donovan and ran over to her, his face full of concern. "What happened?"

My jealousy raged, but I pushed it down. I had no reason to feel that way. We'd completed our bond, and they were friends. Of course, he cared that she was injured. But despite my rational thinking, a little anger still flared.

"I was scoping out the area for a place for Jade and me to train." She turned to me, wincing. "And I got attacked."

"Who attacked you?" That made no sense, but I couldn't deny her wound was real. I tapped into my senses but found nothing.

"It had to be the witch." Mindy leaned against Egan. "She had caramel hair and sable eyes and was asking where our thunder is."

That sounded like my former roommate, but she'd found us fast—before the rest of us had gotten here. "How the hell did she know where to find us?"

"She did see us packed up when we were leaving," Egan said as he touched Mindy's shoulder, examining her wound. "She probably guessed this is where we were rushing off to since we were leaving with the wolf shifters."

Lillith rubbed a hand down her face. "She's smart. She would've been watching in the shadows, waiting to strike."

"Where did she go?" Draco stood between Egan and me protectively. "Maybe we can find her."

"She attacked me, and just as I went to retaliate, she vanished." Mindy placed her head on my mate's shoulder.

I couldn't hold back the rage. It was one thing for her to be hurt and us paying more attention to her, but she was totally using this to touch my mate. My hands fisted, and I took a deep breath, trying to keep a level head. "That's what happened at the cabin," I said, forcing the words through clamped teeth.

Yup, ignoring her proximity to my mate wasn't happening.

Egan pried himself away from her and took a few steps away. "We need to get you back and clean your wound."

"Yeah, okay." She pouted and countered his movement, trying to get close to him again.

Roxy snagged her uninjured arm, keeping her from my mate. "It's a good thing the wound is superficial."

If I hadn't loved the spunky redhead before, I did now. She might love giving people shit, but she was as loyal as they came.

"Ow!" Mindy sniffled. "Even if it's my good arm, it still pulls on the other shoulder."

"Good thing you have shifter healing speed. You'll be back to normal in a few hours," Lillith said, calling her out on the way she was acting worse than it was.

I'm sorry she tried taking advantage of the situation. I

won't let it happen again. Egan took my hand, pulling me close to his side.

With him away from her and next to me, my dragon relaxed. "Let's head back and get settled."

I realized I wouldn't be heading back to Kortright any time soon. I'd worked so hard to go to college, and not even a semester in, I was getting pulled out. Worst of all, I had no one to blame but myself.

Hey, what's wrong? Egan asked as we headed back toward the houses.

Just realized we're probably taking the rest of the semester off. Would they let me come back next semester since I was a scholarship kid? I doubted it, but if we went back, someone might get hurt, especially if Vera continued to hunt me.

This happened last semester too. Egan frowned. *Unfortunately, our life is a little chaotic. Once we get rid of this threat, things should calm down.* I sensed his guilt.

I hated that I'd made him feel that way. That hadn't been my intention. *I wouldn't change a thing if I had the chance.* I looked into his eyes, wanting him to know I meant what I said.

He kissed my forehead. *Good, because I could never let you go.*

"And we get to see new mates drool all over each other again," Lillith complained behind us.

"You're just jealous," Katherine teased.

"I am. Why can't vampires have mates?" she asked dejectedly.

The entire way home, Lillith and Katherine talked about us like we weren't even there.

EGAN BROUGHT the last of our bags into our room and placed them on the floor. "Mindy gave up and headed back to the house with the vampires."

We were staying in an upstairs bedroom of Sadie and Donovan's three-bedroom house. Mindy had tried staying with us, but Egan and Draco had thought it was best if the warrior stayed with us instead of the teacher. Mindy had said she'd been the last one to get hurt, but Lillith had pointed out that it was because she'd gone off into the woods alone. So she was staying with the vampires and Ollie in the blue house on the corner. Roxy and Axel got to keep their home to themselves.

Lilith had drawn the sigils at every exit in all our houses to protect us from the witch's prying eyes. As long as we stayed indoors, we'd be relatively safe.

Draco was staying in the room across the hall from us with Sadie and Donovan staying in their bedroom downstairs. Our room felt homey and was at least three times the size of the one I had back at Sarah's.

The walls were light beige, and a set of windows overlooked the woods. A large, king-sized bed sat in the center, covered in light gray sheets and a dark gray comforter and pillows. The headboard, end tables, and chest of drawers were a light wood color that looked almost white. The large closet across from the windows could easily hold four times the amount of clothes I had.

Right across from the bed was the entryway to our own bathroom, and I could see an all-glass stand-up shower from there. The white tile looked clean, like no one had ever walked in it before.

"Hey." Egan wrapped his arms around me, turning me to face him. "You're somewhere else."

"No, I'm here." I enjoyed his warmth. "It's been a very long day, and it's not even dinner time yet."

"That I understand." He kissed my lips.

My hands fisted his hair, and I pulled him lower to deepen the kiss. Even though we'd had sex earlier this morning, it felt like it had been days ago. I slipped my hand under his shirt and ran my hands along his chest. His defined pecs had my body purring.

He leaned over me, laying me flat on the bed as his mouth worked my lips. My dragon roared for more, and I almost came unglued.

His mouth trailed down my neck as his hand cupped my breast, pinching my nipple between his fingers. A moan escaped me as he sucked on my neck.

Desperate to feel him, I unbuttoned his pants and pushed them, along with his underwear, down. I stroked him, and he groaned against my skin.

Jade. His voice sounded like a song. He pulled me upward and removed my shirt and bra, and his mouth immediately began going to work on me. I wiggled my hands between us, and I removed my jeans and panties, desperate to feel him inside me.

He positioned himself between my legs, but I wanted to try something else. I pushed against his chest, and he rose, confusion in his eyes.

"You don't have your shirt off," I said, my voice raspy.

"Oh, okay." He stood and removed his shirt from his body.

My eyes devoured every single inch of him. His body was hard in all the ways a woman wanted and in every way that counted. I flipped over and crawled to the pillows.

His pupils turned to slits as he watched me from behind. *What are you doing?*

Trying a new position.

He moved toward me and climbed behind me.

Never in a million years would I have dreamed that his touch would turn me on this much. He rubbed himself against me, getting into position.

He slowly entered me, going deeper than ever before. He asked, *Are you okay?*

Yes.

He filled me completely, hitting my spot perfectly. I moved underneath him, and he sped up his thrusting. My head grew dizzy as he pounded into me.

A moan left me that was way too loud, but I didn't give a damn. I opened our bond, letting him feel everything I did.

Whatever had him worried was gone, and the friction set my body on fire.

Our bodies moved as one, and we teetered close to the edge. I closed my eyes, enjoying each touch, each stroke, each feel. He leaned forward and bit the side of my neck. An orgasm rocked through us at the same time.

He rolled off me and gathered me into his arms. *I love you,* he whispered in my brain.

I laid my head against his sweaty chest, listening to his heartbeat. *I love you too.* I felt safe and secure there and drifted off to sleep.

THE NEXT MORNING, Egan and I entered the kitchen. Draco, Sadie, Donovan, Axel, and Roxy were already there. Sadie stood in front of the black stove, putting the last of the bacon on a large white plate. She walked past the light beige cabinets to the island where Roxy and Axel sat on high-backed chairs.

Roxy snatched a plate on the end and piled it full of bacon and pancakes. She pointed to the other wolf shifters and me. "You better get your food before the male dragons get theirs. If you wait, there won't be anything left."

If Draco ate like Egan did, that was true. We'd missed dinner last night, and after the others had gone to bed, we'd eaten leftovers. Egan had eaten everything I hadn't touched.

"Grab what you're going to eat," Draco said, gesturing to us. "We need to talk about something important."

Conversations that started like that were usually the very ones I didn't want to have.

CHAPTER TWELVE

K eeping calm, I took a plate and selected a few pancakes and a handful of bacon to place on it. I'd noticed that my appetite increased the stronger my dragon became. "Is something wrong?"

Sadie filled her own plate while frowning. "I think the better question is: Which problem do you want to discuss?"

"Fair point." Draco had many options to choose from: the dying dragon race, a witch hunting us down, a jealous dragon shifter desiring my mate, a falcon shifter that had tried to kill me. I had to stop. The list could go on for a while. I poured a cup of coffee then took a seat at their large round table fit for eight.

Draco licked his lips as he watched Donovan, Axel, and Roxy fill their plates with food. "I'd like to discuss Jade's training."

"My training? Why?" Connecting with my dragon was my first priority. The sooner I could bridge the gap between us, the less of a liability I'd be. Maybe I could help out in a fight instead of getting beat to a bloody pulp.

Draco stood and walked over to the food. "Mindy was attacked while scouring the area."

"Hey!" Roxy grabbed a butter knife from on top of the tub of butter and lifted it at the dragon. "Don't make me hurt you. We get our food first."

Draco's eyebrows shot up comically. "You're kidding."

"No, man." Axel put more bacon on Roxy's plate. "She's not. The best thing to do is wait. The one time Egan got food first, she almost attacked him."

Egan winked at me and chuckled. "True story. She better be glad I'm a gentleman, or it could've gotten ugly."

"Whatever, Egan. At the time, I was your favorite." Roxy eyed the food one more time and glanced at her plate. "I guess that's enough."

Yeah, I didn't believe that for a minute. If anything, Sadie had been his favorite. I'd been jealous of their relationship, although I hated to admit it now. It was not my proudest moment. I'd been pushing him away, and Sadie was his best friend. Of course, he would talk to her.

"In other words, all dragons are allowed to eat now." Donovan rolled his eyes and joined me at the table. "If it wasn't for Sadie, we wouldn't be as tolerant of you."

"Dude, she's my mate." Axel sat next to his best friend. "You'd still have to tolerate her since I'm stuck with her." An evil grin flitted across his face as he watched the redhead's reaction.

"Stuck with me?" She dropped her plate, and it clanged on the table. "Is that what you want to call it? I'll show you stuck with me tonight."

Axel's eyes twinkled with mirth. "Am I in trouble? Will you have to teach me—"

"Oh, dear God." Donovan closed his eyes and cringed.

"Please do not talk dirty in front of us. I've told you how uncomfortable it makes everyone."

Sadie laughed, sliding between Donovan and me, and scolded, "You know, reacting like that only encourages them."

I smiled so big my cheeks hurt. Despite all the shit we were going through, this group could make me forget about it for a few minutes.

You're breathtaking when you smile like that. Egan slipped onto the seat next to me and placed his hand on my leg. His plate was overflowing with pancakes and bacon.

Sadie had cooked at least five pounds of bacon, and that was a conservative estimate. The salty smell was as intoxicating as the taste. I took a bite and almost moaned. *You're not too bad yourself.*

"Um ..." Draco sat next to Egan like he was afraid to get near Roxy. "I hate to change the subject." The smell of his lie hit us hard.

Roxy gagged and waved her hand in front of her nose. "No lying while eating. That's the ultimate sin."

"Sorry." He cringed. "I was trying to be polite, but I would like to pivot away from this conversation, especially since I want to talk about something serious."

"I'm on board with that suggestion. Please, proceed." Donovan stabbed a pancake and devoured it.

"Like I was saying ..." Draco lifted a hand. "I don't think it's wise for you and Mindy to go off like that on your own. We need to stay close in case something happens."

Egan tensed. "You're right. The sigils don't work outside."

I wouldn't let them take this away from me. "I need to train. I need to be able to protect myself."

"It's an easy solution." Draco tapped his chest. "I'll go with you."

Egan nodded. "And me."

"No." I didn't want to hurt his feelings, but that wasn't a smart idea. "I can't concentrate with you around."

My mate started. "How?"

"Oh, bless his heart." Roxy blew out a breath. "What she's tactfully saying is that Mindy will be salivating all over you the entire time, and the training sessions won't be very productive."

Okay, obviously I wasn't being as coy as I'd hoped.

Egan's focus pivoted to me, and he asked, "Is that true? Is that the only reason you don't want me there?"

There was no way out of this, and the truth would come out one way or another. "Yes, but it's not your fault." I hated that I sounded so insecure.

She means nothing to me. I need you to know that. Egan tightened his hand on my leg like that would reassure me.

You grew up with her. Of course, she means something, but I know she's not a threat. Still, it bothers me that she doesn't respect our relationship. Saying it out loud made me realize that was the problem. I understood how she would be smitten with him—hell, I was too—but her blatant disregard of me was too much.

You're right. I'll talk to her. More guilt wafted from him.

That pissed me off even more. He wasn't encouraging her in the least, but she kept persisting. He had nothing to feel bad about. Either way, he didn't need to handle this problem. *No, I'll talk to her. This is between her and me anyway.*

Sadie cleared her throat, aware that Egan and I were talking through our mind link. "Our entire pack is at your disposal. I can ask a few of our strongest to watch over them too. They can look out from the tree line so they don't inter-fere with the session. That way, if something happens, they can link with the entire pack, and you'll have backup quickly."

"That would work," Draco agreed.

Someone knocked on the front door before opening it. The smell of Mindy and Ollie hit me hard.

"Someone is making themselves feel at home," Roxy grumbled through a mouthful of food.

The two of them joined us in the kitchen, Mindy's eyes glued on Egan. She wore a skintight, light orange shirt that emphasized her breasts along with tight jeans. "Hey. I didn't realize we were having breakfast here."

"We weren't," Roxy said bluntly. "Sadie cooked for everyone in her house, and Axel and I showed up in time to get in."

Sadie smiled. "I can make more if you two haven't eaten."

Mindy chuckled nervously. "No, we ate before coming here."

Ollie ran his fingers through his thin hair, making it look like a nest. His scrawny frame looked awkward in its over-sized black shirt and baggy sweatpants. He had to be wearing borrowed clothes. "Sorry to barge in."

"The front door was unlocked." Mindy fluffed her hair. "I figured it'd be okay with it being a pack neighborhood and all."

I'd hoped to enjoy breakfast before seeing her, but fate had other plans. I finished my pancake and set my fork down.

"Good, you're almost done." Mindy stepped backward awkwardly. "Are you ready to train?"

"Yes." I needed to connect with my dragon soon so she'd

leave. We'd have to find a way to get her back to the thunder safely.

Draco finished the bacon on his plate. "We were just discussing that. I was telling the others that I don't think it's safe for you and her to go into the woods alone, so some wolves and I will be joining you."

"You can't come," Mindy said hastily.

Egan shifted in his seat. "Why not? After the witch attacked you, it makes sense to have protection."

Mindy inhaled sharply. "Since Jade is older and I haven't worked with a changed dragon before, I'm worried that other dragons could influence her own. She wasn't born with her dragon, so she's not as acclimated to it as most of the students I teach."

"Then we can have more wolves around instead, and you two can train in the clearing at the other end of the neighborhood, right behind some houses. It isn't isolated like the other location." Sadie tried to sound upbeat, but it fell a little flat.

"Fine." Mindy didn't seem thrilled, but she didn't argue. "But no dragons lurking nearby. Are you ready to go?"

"Sure." I didn't want to spend any time with her, but if this would help me, I could deal. I drained the rest of my coffee, needing the caffeine to get through the morning. Egan and I had reconnected several times throughout the night, so I was a little groggy, but I'd gladly sacrifice my sleep again.

"If anything seems odd, let me know." Egan kissed me. *And that goes for her too.*

I love you. And to think I'd stupidly fought our connection. *I'll let you know immediately if something is off.*

Donovan stood and finished his orange juice. After kissing Sadie, he waved for Mindy and me to follow him.

"I'll take you to the clearing Sadie was talking about and introduce you to the wolves that will keep an eye on you. I need to check on someone down there anyway."

The three of us headed out the front door and walked through the neighborhood in silence. I didn't know Donovan that well, and he wasn't the most talkative person I'd ever met. He wasn't stand-offish, per se, but he was hard to read at times, unless it was regarding Sadie. The love he felt for her was evident in every way.

Even though I had a lot to say to Mindy, I hoped the training would give us time to bond, and maybe she'd back off without me needing to address it. I didn't want there to be any awkwardness between us, especially since we were part of the same thunder. If she was in love with Egan, it would be hard to see him with someone else, so maybe she needed time. At least, that was what I kept telling myself when it came to her.

The walk through the neighborhood was nice. The sun was high in a cloudless sky. The cool breeze felt pleasant on my hot shifter skin. After walking past fifty houses, we reached a large section of open space between several homes and the trees.

Three men stood in front of the curb that led to the clearing, and Donovan nodded as we approached. All three of them looked a few years older than us, probably in their mid-twenties.

The tallest one, who stood on the far left, rubbed his cleft chin. His short, tawny hair contrasted against his light olive skin, giving him a glow. Despite the chill, he wore a sleeveless white shirt that revealed his muscular arms. "Are these the two we need to watch?"

"Yeah, and if the witch or anyone else shows up, let me know." Donovan glanced at me. "You going to be okay?"

I tried to sound confident as I said, "I'll be fine."

"Let's get to work." Mindy marched over to the clearing without waiting.

I hurried to catch up, not wanting her to think I already couldn't hack it. I glanced over my shoulder, but the three guys were already gone. When Donovan had said they'd keep out of sight, he'd meant it. If it hadn't been for their faint scent in the air, I wouldn't have known they were around.

"First, we need to get you to connect with your dragon. Then we can try to access your power." Mindy tossed her hair over her shoulder and lifted her chin.

"Sounds great." I was willing to do whatever it took to embrace my new life. "So how do we begin?"

"Have you ever really tried intertwining yourself with your dragon?"

"I'm guessing no since I'm not sure what that means." I'd only ever felt my dragon when she was angry.

"Oh God." She blew out her breath in disgust. "I'll have to go super basic with you."

"Yes." I couldn't keep my annoyance from slipping through. "I've only been part dragon for a week now."

She waved her hand at me. "That's part of the problem. You think of yourself as part human and part dragon."

"That's wrong?" I'd seen Egan and Draco shift. When they were dragons, they were pure beasts. I wasn't sure how else to consider it.

"Of course it's wrong," she said condescendingly. "You aren't half and half. Your human and dragon sides are one and the same. You can't think of them as separate beings."

"So I think of myself as both?" That seemed strange because, in my mind, I considered them completely separate.

She crossed her arms and looked at the sky. "You'll see what I mean. Just try connecting with your dragon."

"How?" If she was a teacher; shouldn't she provide more guidance?

"That's not something I can help with." She held her arms outward. "We all connect with our dragons differently. You just have to figure it out."

All right, that wasn't very helpful. I took a deep breath to calm myself and closed my eyes, but I didn't sense anything inside me.

I searched deep within myself, and after God knew how long, something flickered inside—a warmth that I latched on to and tugged.

As soon as I did, a raging inferno slammed into me. I tried crying out for help but couldn't.

CHAPTER THIRTEEN

The flames flicked throughout my body like never before. It had gone from nothing to a fiery temperature within seconds, terrifying me. I was out of control, and I wasn't sure how the hell to calm down.

"Are you okay?" Mindy asked, sounding genuinely concerned.

Unable to verbalize anything, I jerked my head from side to side helplessly.

She touched my arm and yanked her hand back. "You're hot. You must have found your dragon, and she's overtaking you. Push it down and away. Don't let her get the upper hand."

I wanted to yell, "How the hell am I supposed to do that?" But I couldn't do anything.

Egan's voice popped into my head. *Jade, are you under attack?*

Great, I didn't want him to be worried about me. I had enough on my plate without stressing over him. *I'm struggling to connect with my dragon, but I'm fine.* At least, I hoped I was.

"Get a handle on her," Mindy said with urgency.

Trying to push everything from my mind, I concentrated on the flames. I shut down the link between Egan and me, not needing any distractions. Knowing him, he'd be rushing to me right now, but I'd address that after I got control over my dragon. He couldn't see me struggling.

I tried to center myself. I'd learned in martial arts that letting your fear take hold meant you couldn't think or act rationally and your fear could take on a life of its own. I wanted to latch on to the flames instead of squash them, but maybe my dragon was trying to tempt me.

Maybe Mindy was right—I shouldn't consider each part as separate, but that was exactly what they felt like.

Ignoring the urge to embrace the flames, I continued to breathe in a steady rhythm, and after several long minutes, the fire receded. I wasn't safe yet. The flames could erupt again without much effort.

Mindy touched my arm again. "You're cooling down."

Her stating the obvious irritated me, but at least, she was concerned about me, and I didn't want to ruin the moment.

"Uh-huh." That was all I could manage since I was still focused on keeping my breathing and heartbeat steady.

"Good, keep doing that."

Her command irritated me, but I couldn't let her get to me.

The flames didn't appear to be a threat anymore, so I opened my eyes and found Mindy staring toward the neighborhood.

I turned and found Egan running toward me with Draco right behind.

Egan's eyes glowed bright, especially against his dark gray shirt, and his pupils were slits. He raced directly to me and placed his hands on my shoulders, scanning me from head to toe. "Are you hurt?"

Mindy placed a hand on her hip. "Don't be so dramatic. She lost control, that's all."

"She was scared," Egan bit out without looking at her. He cupped my face and lowered his forehead against mine. His breath hit my face, which surprisingly didn't smell like bacon.

"I'm fine." I shut my eyes, enjoying his touch. I always found comfort in him.

Draco stepped next to me and asked, "What happened?"

"She was trying to connect with her dragon, and it didn't go over well," Mindy answered for me. "But she's fine. She got it under control ... eventually."

The way she'd worded that got under my skin. It was like she was slighting me, but hell, I'd failed miserably and probably deserved it.

"She hasn't been a dragon long." Egan took a deep breath like he was smelling me. "She's the youngest one you've ever trained. You should probably take that into consideration."

"I'm sorry. I've never trained a former human before. The last instructor who trained a former human is dead, so no trainer alive has that experience. And from the sounds of it, your mother didn't struggle like Jade." She huffed.

Now that the adrenaline had left my body, my legs felt weak, but I didn't want Egan to know, so I forced myself to stand strong. "It's fine. She and I can figure this out together." I didn't need Egan discouraging her and causing her not to want to help me.

He frowned. "But—"

"I'll be fine." I kissed his lips and forced a smile.

"Thank you for checking on me." It shocked me at times how much he cared about me. He was the kindest and most handsome man I'd ever met. I couldn't believe he was all mine.

"I will never not check on you," he breathed, his eyes penetrating my soul.

"Good." I kissed him again, not ready for him to go. *I love you.*

"I love you too." He said the words out loud for everyone to hear. "I think that's enough for today. Let's get you home."

"No, I want to try again." I had to get a handle on my dragon in order to feel stronger and more secure. I could also be a stronger force against the witch instead of a liability. "I mean if Mindy is okay with it."

"Sure, we've only been out here thirty minutes," Mindy said, digging at my failure even more.

Egan frowned, not happy with my decision. *You're tired. I feel it through our bond.*

I couldn't lie to him even if I wanted to. *I'll be fine. I'll rest for a few minutes, but I really want to try one more time, if I can find my strength.*

Jade—

I'm not asking for permission. I loved him wholeheartedly, and I understood that he was coming from a place of love and concern, but it was my decision, not his.

His shoulders shook with quiet laughter. *I understand how Donovan and Axel feel with strong-willed mates. I always thought they were overbearing, but it's easy to do when someone means so much to you.*

I reminded myself that he wasn't trying to control me. I'd lived with a controlling, manipulative aunt who'd acted, not out of concern but a desire for power. I'd promised myself when I'd run away from Sarah that no one would ever make decisions for me again.

"Fine." He took a step back and looked at Draco. "But we stay here."

"No, not happening," Mindy interjected loudly. "She almost lost complete control with only my dragon near. We can't chance having any more nearby."

"I'll be okay," I reassured him again. I understood why he didn't want to leave. If he'd felt even a smidgen of the fear that had overtaken me, I couldn't blame him one bit. But I couldn't let fear dictate my life.

"Are you sure that our presence would cause a problem?" Draco questioned, sounding skeptical.

"Look, I'm not sure." Mindy straightened her shoulders and grimaced, probably from her injury. "But the fewer variables, the better."

"She's right. I'll let you know if I need you. I promise." And if I lost control again, I didn't want Egan to see. He was upset enough just knowing I'd struggled.

"Be careful." He brushed his knuckles against my cheek and headed back toward the house.

Mindy scoffed. "Let's hope you can at least connect with your dragon for a second."

Yeah, I hoped so too.

When Egan was out of sight, I searched for her again, but I couldn't find a spark. All I felt was cold. Only a day into training, and I was already failing.

THE NEXT WEEK passed in a blur. Every morning, Mindy and I would train, but I was making less and less progress. I couldn't even find my dragon anymore.

I almost talked to Egan about it, but he was my safe space. When I was with him, the bad faded away, and I didn't want to lose that. Mindy was helping me despite her desire for Egan, but her frustration was deepening my depression.

"Here's some food." Egan placed a plate of biscuits, sausage, and eggs in front of me, along with a large steaming cup of coffee. "Do you need anything else?"

"No." My appetite had been nonexistent lately, despite things being great with Egan.

"You need to eat up," Egan encouraged as Mindy entered the kitchen with Ollie right behind. "You have training again all morning."

Ever since that first morning, Mindy and Ollie had always come over to eat with us.

"Yeah, like that'll help her," Mindy snickered.

"Isn't the student a reflection of the teacher?" Roxy asked, banging her shoulder into Mindy as she walked by. "And you sound like you're enjoying her struggle." She slid into the seat next to mine, staring the dragon down.

Surprisingly, the dragon didn't respond, but not even Roxy standing up for me could make me feel better. I couldn't do a damn thing right, and I was failing Egan.

Egan's shoulders tensed. "Mindy, I'd like to have a word with you."

"Of course." She batted her eyes at him. "Right now?"

"Now." He walked past her into the living room.

He hadn't been around her any more than he had to be, but my jealousy simmered below the surface. Why did he want to talk to her? Maybe he'd realized she was a better dragon than me.

My heart pounded as the two of them walked out the front door. I was being completely irrational, but I couldn't stand not knowing what they were talking about. I stood from the table and glanced at the people in the kitchen. "Uh ..." I almost lied but caught myself in time. They could guess what I was about to do, but I didn't need to flaunt it. "I need to go do something."

"Yeah, girl, you do." Roxy nodded. "That bitch wants your man."

Sadie glared at her best friend and said, "You know he—"

"Just let her do what she needs to do." Donovan smiled at me with understanding, his dark blue eyes lightening. "You've never had to struggle with feeling insecure about connecting with your animal," he gently reminded his mate.

"You're right." Sadie motioned to the door. "You'll feel better if you listen anyway."

Axel winked. "Your secret is safe with us."

Ollie was the only one who hadn't given me their blessing even though I hadn't been asking for it.

"Hey, you can tell me what to do." He gestured to the bracelet in my jeans pocket. "You have insurance."

Not wanting to waste any more time, I hurried into the living room and placed my ear to the front door. Discretion was pointless since everyone already knew what I was doing.

"You're discouraging her," Egan said with malice. "I thought you were better than that."

Mindy replied in a softer, almost girly voice, "Look, she's struggling. Maybe she's not the right mate for you."

"You've got to be kidding." Egan sounded shocked. "She's my fated mate."

"Sometimes, fate gets it wrong. Why should humans be our mates? We're strong and aren't liabilities like them ...

like *her*. We can go back to the arrangement our parents made."

My anger burned inside. She was trying to talk my mate out of being with me. We might not be friends, but I thought we'd established a civil relationship. Obviously, I'd been wrong, and she only wanted to appease me to make a play at Egan.

His words were strong and final as he said, "All I want is her. If you think there is an ounce of me who contemplates the thought of you, there is not. She is the most important person in my life, and I'll give up anyone or anything that tries to come between us."

"You can't be serious." Her voice shook. "She's weak, Egan. You need someone strong beside you, especially for what's ahead."

"I'm strongest with her next to me, and you need to realize that helping her is the only way to salvage any type of friendship between us."

Tears burned in my eyes that he'd stood up for me. I couldn't believe I'd doubted him for a second.

His footsteps headed back to the house.

Dammit, I needed to get away from the door. I didn't want to see Mindy's enjoyment if she caught me eavesdropping. I rushed back into the kitchen.

Right as I slid into my seat, Egan entered the room. Everyone stared at him, and he paused beside me.

Roxy arched an eyebrow. "I take it things didn't go well outside."

"No, things did not." Egan kissed my forehead and pointed to my food. "And you haven't eaten anything."

"I'm not hungry." Especially not after overhearing Mindy's desperate pleas.

"Good." Mindy appeared in the threshold, avoiding Egan's gaze. "Let's go train."

"Maybe I should go with you." Draco stood and took a step toward the front door.

"We've already gone through this. It needs to be just her and me." She waved me on. "Let's get a move on. "

Gladly. I didn't want her anywhere near my mate. I kissed Egan's lips for longer than necessary. Maybe I was being petty, but I was reinforcing my claim on him. Stupid harlot.

Egan wrapped an arm around my waist and kissed me deeper. *It's sexy that you want her to see us together and stake your claim, especially after what you heard out there.*

I stiffened. *You knew I was listening?*

He kissed my nose. *I'd be upset if you hadn't been, but let me know if she does anything funny. I love you.*

I love you too. I turned to find Mindy watching us with a frown on her face.

When I'd caught her, she quickly smoothed her face like that would fool me. She marched to the door, and I grabbed my bag with an extra change of clothes I was certain I wouldn't need and followed closely behind.

As we stepped into the clearing, Mindy crossed her arms and stared me down.

I wasn't sure what she wanted me to do, so I stood there and stared back. Anger bubbled, but I held it at bay. Connecting with my dragon was more important than how I felt about her.

She rolled her eyes and waved her hand. "Go for it. Try to reach her."

The urge to slap her flitted through me, but I closed my eyes to center myself. Getting upset would distract me from the task at hand. I didn't know how long I stood there, but all I found was the same coldness from the past few days.

"I really hope you start doing better, for Egan's sake," Mindy said hatefully.

"What are you talking about?" I hadn't expected for her to come right out and say something like this to me, but I guessed after Egan's rejection, she wanted to give me a go.

"Do you really think a strong dragon like him needs a weak-ass dragon—" She sneered. "Let's be real, you're really just a human since you can't even feel your dragon anymore. Do you think our thunder will accept a weakling like you?"

Anger flared inside me, and the flames that had been dormant for days spurred to life. "I'm going to connect with my dragon if it's the last thing I do." I gritted my teeth, and my breathing increased.

Her eyes widened. "You're losing control again. You need to calm the flames within."

Shit, here I was, regressing even more, but my anger grew, and there was no reining it in.

Egan stepped from the trees, glaring at her, and growled, "What the fuck did you say to her?"

CHAPTER FOURTEEN

The animosity flowing off Egan pulled my attention from within and onto him. Egan had cursed? The flames dimmed as my anger tempered to a worried state for my mate. I'd never seen him act this way, so something had to be horribly wrong.

"What are you doing here?" Mindy whispered with dread.

I must have missed something. I scanned the clearing to determine what happened.

Egan marched over and took my hand as he stared Mindy down. He sneered, his expression morphing into one of pure rage. "Curious about your methods. You see, I had an interesting conversation with Mom yesterday while you two were training. Between that and your antics this morning, I wondered why you were adamant not to have me or Draco near."

"I told you why." Mindy's shrill voice hurt my ears. "We didn't need any distractions." Her cheeks turned pink, either from embarrassment or anger.

"The fact that you're telling the truth speaks volumes.

You didn't want any distractions. Distractions from you sabotaging my mate from connecting with her animal. How could you do that to her?" Smoke trickled from his flared nostrils, and he protectively stepped in front of me.

All of the dots connected. "Wait. You haven't been helping me?" I shouldn't have been shocked, but I was.

"I—" Mindy's mouth dropped like she wasn't sure what to say.

"All this time, you're the reason I was struggling. You made me feel like a failure." Rage coursed through me at the betrayal. My heart pounded, and my breathing turned ragged.

"You have to understand it's nothing personal. I'm just the better fit for Egan." Mindy lifted her hands as if in surrender, though her words declared war.

"Nothing personal?" She was crazier than I'd ever imagined. "That's the very definition of personal. He's my mate."

"Of course, someone like *you* wouldn't understand."

"What? Someone who isn't delusional?" And I'd thought the human world was cruel. She was on the same level as my aunt.

She waved a hand at me. "You're just a broken girl who somehow got mated to the strongest dragon in the world."

"Okay, you've said more than enough," Egan hissed and tried blocking me from her view.

"Yeah, protect her since she can't defend herself." Mindy's eyes narrowed as she sidestepped to look at me. "You're lucky he's standing between us."

"First off, no one cares or wants to hear your opinion." Egan's body quivered with unbridled anger. "Secondly, she's stronger than you have ever been. What kind of dragon runs and hides when her own kind is under attack?"

Mindy straightened her shoulders. "Please, like you

were even at risk. Maybe if you hadn't run off to some stupid college, we'd be mated and the attack never would've happened."

Egan rasped, "Jade was made for me, and I refuse to contemplate a life without her. You need to get that through your brain."

Mindy lifted her chin in defiance. "It's a good thing you're handsome since you're obviously not very smart."

Did she think it was okay to say stuff like that? Flames flickered throughout my body at her audacity. "You made me think I was broken and that the thunder wouldn't accept me. Now you're going so far as to insult me and my mate."

"They shouldn't accept you," she smirked. "I should be with him. He needs someone strong."

The bitch was about to see strong. "You don't get to decide. He does." I let go of Egan's hand and walked around him. I refused to let him protect me. If this girl thought I was weak, I'd prove her wrong. "And he chose me. He's told you that repeatedly, so I'm thinking you're the one who's dumb."

"You can't talk to me that way, you stupid—"

I punched her right in the jaw. A loud crunch sounded as her head jerked to the side, and she collapsed.

The raging inferno inside me prevented me from doing anything else as it took on a life of its own. Arms wrapped around me and turned me toward a strong chest. My mate's face grew concerned as he watched me.

"We need to focus on you. You will lose control if we don't fix the problems she's caused." Egan's fingers brushed my cheek, but the usual comfort it provided was missing.

My dragon was angry and refused to not be heard, even with Egan trying to soothe us.

Footsteps pounded, and Draco said, "Get her away from here. I'll handle Mindy."

I wanted to finish the bitch, because breaking her jaw hadn't been enough, but I needed to take care of myself.

"Fine." He sighed. "But my conversation with her isn't over. She went too damn far."

I forced the next words through my thoughts, even though I didn't want to, but I refused to be that girl. I could work on myself while he did what he needed to. *If you need to talk to her—*

You will always be my first and most important priority. I'm just livid she did this to you. He scooped me up in his arms and took off toward the woods, barely jarring me.

I hadn't realized I couldn't walk until he'd picked me up. Every ounce of my self-control was consumed with trying not to implode. The more my anger festered, the more out of control it got.

He ran so fast my hair whipped around my face, and the air felt amazing. Between that and his touch, the flames receded slightly.

I'm going to put you down. I think this place will work.

He placed me gently on the ground, but I kept my eyes closed, staying in his embrace. The flames grew hotter without the breeze. *I ... I don't know what to do.* I tried pushing the dragon back like Mindy had told me, but it only enraged her more. She didn't relent, and I found myself retreating instead.

Those flames, you need to grab on to them, Egan said soothingly.

But they're so hot. I didn't feel the tug to connect with them like I had on my first day of training. *They'll burn me.*

No, they won't, Egan growled, annoyance wafting off him.

He'd never treated me like this, and it hurt. Out of all the times, now was when he'd be disappointed. *Okay, I'll try. Just be patient with me.*

Oh, baby, I am. I'm not upset with you. I'm angry with Mindy. She's been pushing you to this point all week, and I should've known. He kissed my forehead. *But I need you to trust me and grasp the flames. Don't hide or fight them. Your dragon is pissed because she's been trying to connect with you and you've rejected her.*

That was why she'd gone cold and I couldn't find her. She'd been hurt.

Pushing away my terror, I steadied myself and opened myself up to the flames. The flames licked against my mind, challenging me, but I held steady. After God knew how long, the urge to connect with the flames overcame me again.

I didn't hesitate. I should've trusted my instincts from the very beginning.

My dragon pushed forward, and I winced, ready for the pain, but the contact didn't hurt. She melded with me, and I stepped from Egan's arms and looked at the world around me. I thought my vision had been crystal clear after we'd bonded, but now I saw colors I'd never seen before. I had no clue what to consider them, but they were breathtaking.

As our minds blended together, immense power shot through me. My skin prickled as my body began to expand. I hadn't considered the possibility of shifting, and I pulled back from my dragon. She hissed and locked on more tightly.

You need to shift, Egan said reassuringly. *It's the best way to connect with your dragon half. Don't hold back. Let her take hold.*

Okay, I was willing to try. I didn't feel as overwhelmed now but rather more unsure of the unknown.

Here, take this. If I shifted, I didn't want to lose the broken bracelet we needed to keep a leash on Ollie. My hands shook as I pulled it out and placed it in Egan's pocket.

He nodded. *I'll take care of it. Just connect with her.*

She clamped tighter, and my bones shifted, but thankfully, it didn't hurt. Egan and Draco had made it look so easy, so natural, and now I understood why. My bones weren't breaking but rather moving and changing. Something sprouted from my back, ripping my clothes. Large boney wings stretched out.

I watched as my skin changed into olive scales a few shades lighter than Egan's. I was at least twice as tall and took up a quarter of the large clearing.

Egan stepped in front of me, smiling tenderly. *You're just as gorgeous in your dragon form as you are in your other one.*

His words did something to the beast inside, and a soft purr escaped. She'd been worried he wouldn't approve of her.

It surprised me that I understood her emotions, thoughts, and needs perfectly, even though she was a beast. She was part of me, not an entirely separate entity.

I'll be right back, Egan said and rushed toward a section of woods. *I'm going to strip down and shift with you.*

Just as I was about to ask why he didn't strip down here, a branch broke a few steps away. I turned, realizing we weren't alone; the musky scent told me wolf shifters were near.

It had to be the three shifters Donovan had instructed to watch us. I felt better knowing we had backup. The witch had been silent for a week, but she'd eventually grow tired of waiting.

The three wolves peeked through the tree branches, taking in my animal form.

It dawned on me that they'd probably seen me naked. *Please tell me they didn't see anything when I shifted.*

Maybe, but if they did, it wasn't for long. Egan stepped out from the woods in all his naked glory. His body began to change right before my eyes. *They're shifters, so nudity is nothing new to them. Don't be embarrassed. I just didn't want to destroy my clothes since I don't have a spare outfit.*

That was kind of sad. It would have been nice to see him naked for a while. It startled me that I enjoyed watching my mate shift into his dragon. Watching the change was intoxicating.

The beast within me was excited. This was the first time they'd meet. *I'm hearing you say that you have no problem with other men seeing me naked.*

His wings sprouted, and his pupils turned to slits. He growled deeply, *I did not say that, but there are times when that may happen, even if I'd rather it not. You don't want me to be jealous and rip our friends' heads off, do you?*

I felt truly free and strong. I teased, *Maybe. It might make me feel special.*

Don't tempt me, Jade. His dragon stepped toward me, his face caressing the side of mine.

Please tell me we can fly. The urge to take to the air and have the wind underneath me dug into me. I'd been jealous of Ollie as I'd watched him fly the other day, and I was finally in a position to experience it.

It's daytime, so we have to be careful. Only a quick, low spin around the neighborhood; then we come back here. If you want to do a longer flight, we'll need to do it at night.

Egan stepped back and spread his wings, about to take to the air.

Deal. I realized was clueless. *Uh ... do I just flap and it works?*

Don't overthink it. Let your dragon handle that part. His body lifted into the air.

That sounded easier said than done, but he hadn't led me astray. I looked skyward, and my dragon took charge. My wings moved slowly at first, hovering me off the ground. Then they moved stronger and stronger, and soon I was higher than the trees.

Egan took off toward Sadie and Donovan's home, and as we flew over the neighborhood, a few kids pointed at us and waved.

Flying as a dragon felt as natural as walking. I twirled around, enjoying the surrounding freedom.

Lillith, Katherine, and Ollie were outside, sitting in the sunlight outside the homes we were staying at. They all smiled as they watched Egan and me move in rhythm with each other, flying around and playing.

My dragon was happy and at peace, almost purring. All too soon, Egan led us back to the clearing, our time in the air done. Tonight, I'd be begging him to go out again.

Right as we descended into the clearing, something cold and sinister brushed against me. My body tensed, and I spun around, looking for the apparition.

Of course, now would be when the witch returned. She disappeared for a while, probably wanting us to lower our guard. It had worked since she'd been the furthest thing from my mind. *Egan, the witch.*

Where? He surveyed the area for her in physical form.

No, she's projecting. I flew higher to get a better vantage, but I saw nothing out of sorts. Maybe my mind was playing tricks on me.

Let's land and shift back. We need to get back to the house where we'll be protected. He flew down to the ground and shifted back into his human form.

When I landed, I took a deep breath, unsure how to initiate the change back to two legs. My dragon was still stuck in my mind, so I did the only thing I could think of: I asked her, *Please, help me shift back.*

Instead of fighting me, she withdrew inwardly. The more she pulled away, the smaller my body became. Back on two legs, I ran toward the trees to hide. I'd forgotten that I didn't have any clothes handy.

Fully dressed, Egan stepped into the clearing. *I'll go ask a wolf near the training grounds to get your bag and bring it to me.*

Draco appeared through the branches, looking frantic. He carried the bag I'd stashed nearby for when I shifted. He handed it to Egan. "Here, get her dressed quickly. We have a problem."

Great, I had a feeling I knew exactly who, or rather what it was.

CHAPTER FIFTEEN

"Let me take a wild guess; Mindy is involved," Egan said, clutching the bag, and turned to me.

We were thinking along the same lines. The wolves' scent was getting closer, and I wrapped my arms around myself. I doubted they were as close as it felt, but with my stronger nose, it smelled like they were right on top of me. I was tempted to cover my private parts with leaves.

"Yes, but are you surprised?" The maliciousness dripping from Draco's words shocked me.

I hadn't spent much time with him since I was either training or exhausted from training, but like Ollie, he didn't say much. I figured it was due to their natures, but not being part of the core group didn't help. Even though Sadie and the others always included Draco, I was sure he felt on the outskirts of their close bonds.

That was the thing with this group. They were fiercely loyal and protected the ones they cared about.

Maybe if I tried pulling Draco in more and talking, we'd get to know him better. After all, he was here, risking his life for us. I'd been depressed about my dragon, and Egan had been working hard to keep that darkness from swallowing me whole. I could make more of an effort with Draco now.

"No, not at all," Egan said curtly. "She's probably trying to scare us so I won't stay mad at her."

Even if you don't stay pissed at her, I will. I couldn't easily forgive her deception. Not only had she tried to hurt me, but she'd also made me look like I couldn't adapt to this world and connect with my dragon. Every show of concern had been to hide her true intent.

I'm beyond pissed. She's lost my trust and my friendship. If I could kick her out of our thunder, I would. Egan hurried over to me, and when he saw me in all my naked glory, he stopped. The anger wafting through our bond dissipated, and the spicy scent of his arousal surrounded me.

It was true what they said: guys had a one-track mind.

My body responded in earnest, calling me out on my hypocrisy. Even though we'd had sex before breakfast, I could easily have gone another round or three with him. Hell, who was I kidding? I could spend days locked in a room with him and never get tired of his hard, sexy body.

A shifter coughed uncomfortably, reminding us that we weren't alone.

If I could have told them to scram, I would have without any hesitation, but we had the witch and Mindy to contend with. *Rain check?*

Only because I don't want to disrespect you like this with all these people around. He wrapped an arm around my waist and set the bag on the ground next to me. A low growl emanated from his chest as he kissed my lips.

You're about to make me beg you to give them a show. His sweet taste filled my mouth, warming my body more. I deepened our kiss, my hormones taking hold.

Egan obliged before groaning as he pulled back and

glanced at his crotch. *You're making this really uncomfortable for me.*

His naughty side made him even more attractive. I never would've guessed until the past few weeks together. I loved that he was only like this with me. I rubbed my hand over him and waggled my eyebrows. *We can't have that. I could help you out.*

He kissed me and grabbed my hand, holding it still. He placed the bracelet in my palm and nipped my lip then stepped back. *I'm doing this because I love you.* He checked me out again, his golden eyes glowing brighter. He was struggling to leave me, and I loved it. *Hurry and get dressed before I change my mind or go crazy with so many guys standing this close to you while you're naked.*

I sighed loudly, letting him know I didn't approve of his decision. I quickly got dressed, put the bracelet back inside my jeans pocket, and headed to where he and Draco waited.

The warrior dragon ran his foot over the grass, averting his gaze from me. He scratched the back of his neck and rolled his shoulders, still uncomfortable. The best way to pretend that Egan and I hadn't almost mauled each other in front of him and the wolves was to steer the conversation in a safer direction. "What did Mindy do?"

"After a few minutes, she ran after you two." Draco surveyed the woods like he expected her to pop up. "But when I chased after her, I couldn't find her."

"Let's hunt her scent." Egan took off toward the other clearing, on a mission.

"That's what I'm trying to tell you," Draco said, causing Egan to stop and return. "She and her scent vanished, and I was only a few steps behind her"

The memory of the cold chill against my arm flitted

through my mind. I'd been sure the witch had been watching us, but after Mindy had just vanished, I worried that the two might be connected. Surely she wouldn't let the witch take her to get Egan to focus on her?

"Dammit. We don't need her doing something stupid." Egan faced the watching wolves. "Can you let Sadie and Donovan know that Mindy is missing and we need help tracking her down?"

"Of course," the taller one said. "We'll shift and circle back." The guy disappeared into the trees, and within seconds, I heard three sets of paws hitting the ground, heading back to the houses.

Flames flicked against my mind, and I partially opened myself to them. My dragon surged forward, loaning me her hearing and eyesight. As I scanned the woods, I could see birds flying and a squirrel running from branch to branch, but I didn't see anything larger than that. "Egan, I felt that cold presence in the air. And now this."

"Let's not jump to conclusions. Let's head back to the house. Maybe she went there to throw Draco off her trail," Egan said and placed his hand on the small of my back, urging me forward.

"I hope that's what she did." Draco didn't sound convinced. "Otherwise, this could be really bad."

Egan sighed. "Let's search before we focus on any other scenarios."

The three of us hurried through the neighborhood, and at our section of houses, Lillith, Katherine, and Ollie were still sitting in front of the light blue house. They waved us over.

Ollie pursed his lips and crossed his arms as he sat back in the seat, giving us a wide berth. The only person he talked to was Mindy, making us more wary of him.

Katherine beamed at me. "We saw you up there flying with Egan. We knew you could do it!"

They were so proud I would've thought they'd accomplished something instead of me. "It was pretty amazing." Despite the potentially dire situation, I couldn't help grinning. I had no doubt that the memory would be one of my favorites.

My happiness was short-lived when Ollie's brows furrowed and he asked, "Where's Mindy?"

Lilith shrugged. "Who cares? She'd only ruin the moment."

I winced. Mindy had tried to make sure that moment never happened, which was way worse.

"That's not a good look. What happened?" Lillith glanced from me to Egan to Draco. When no one responded, she placed her hands on her hips. "I'm assuming a certain blonde, green-eyed monster did something unpleasant."

"Green eyes?" Draco's face wrinkled with confusion. "She doesn't have—"

"It's a saying." Poor guy. They couldn't talk like that around him. He'd only been in our world a week. "*Green-eyed* means jealous."

"Which she clearly is." Lillith narrowed her eyes, daring him to disagree with her.

Katherine patted her friend's shoulder. "I don't think he's disagreeing with you."

"Has she come back here?" Egan nibbled his bottom lip.

Lillith shook her head. "No. Was she supposed to? I thought she was down there with Jade."

The front door to Sadie's house opened, and she and Donovan walked outside with Axel and Roxy right behind.

"I heard the bitch is gone." Roxy's hazel eyes were alight with glee. "I gotta say, I never thought her ass would leave."

"Damn, Roxy." Donovan grimaced. "Tell us how you really feel, why don't you?"

"Oh, I thought I'd made it pretty clear." She lifted a brow, staring him down. "Do you need it spelled out more?"

"You two, stop it." Sadie rolled her eyes and faced us. "Over twenty wolves are searching for Mindy as we speak. No one can find her. It's like she disappeared."

Draco rubbed his forehead. "That's what happened to me too. I was hoping you all could pick up on her scent."

"When we were up in the air, I felt a coldness press against me like back at the dorm when the witch was watching us, and for Mindy to disappear moments before we landed is too suspicious." The witch must have done something to her.

"If you felt a coldness, that means the witch was astral projecting. She couldn't do anything in that state, could she?" Axel ran a hand over his buzzed hair.

Ollie stood and stepped closer, putting his hands in his pockets. "She has strong magic like the powder she gave me to knock Jade out. There's no telling who's working for her. She could've given her something to take her without a trace."

Ugh, this was just lovely. "What do we do? Do you know where the witch is staying?"

"No." Ollie wrung his hands. "Like I said before, she told me as little as possible. I have no clue where she could've taken her."

"We should've known it was too quiet." Lillith scowled. "Instead, we played right into her hand."

Sadie paced. "If witchcraft hid them, we couldn't have

done much. We wouldn't have been able to see her regardless."

"How do we find her?" The longer she was with the witch, the likelier she'd get hurt or give up the thunder.

Roxy crossed her arms. "You really want to find her? I say good riddance."

Maybe Mindy deserved that, but their thunder didn't. "She is someone's daughter and a member of Egan's—" My dragon growled, not happy with me. "My thunder. She's obviously an important teacher there for them to have sent her to help me, and she knows the location of the thunder. Do you think the witch will just give up on Mindy telling her where to find everyone?"

Egan pulled me against his chest and wrapped me in his warm embrace. *I've always known you're an amazing person, but the way you're putting the thunder before the shit she's done to us proves it.*

It isn't easy. I could be honest with him, but if I let Roxy in on that, she'd stir the beast inside. It was enough for her that Mindy had screwed me over.

"Fine, be the bigger person." Roxy stomped her feet dramatically. "And you're right. She'd give up that thunder in a heartbeat."

Sadie's eyes widened at her friend. "Let's hope not. Sometimes, it's best to think before you say whatever pops into your mind."

"Girl, sometimes I don't even know what's going to come out." Roxy waved her hand in front of her mouth. "We're sometimes shocked at the same time, but damn, I always agree with the words."

Lillith snorted. "That's a good thing since you said them."

Roxy nodded. "Fair point. It might get awkward if I didn't."

"Okay." Donovan clapped his hands. "Mindy is with the witch. We need to figure out how the hell to find her."

"The problem is the witch will see us coming since she can keep an eye on those two." Draco pointed at Egan and me.

"I have a suggestion," Ollie said hesitantly.

Lillith tapped her foot. "Which would be?"

"A witch lives an hour away from my cast." He rocked on his heels. "We helped her hide from hunters, and she owes us. She should be able to block the locator spell and maybe find Mindy, though I doubt that will work. But we could try."

The idea of Vera not being able to find us sounded promising. *What are your thoughts?*

I'm not sure, but you have the bracelet. If we could stop Vera from watching our every move whenever we aren't protected, it would take away her advantage. If we can't find Mindy, we may need to go back to the thunder and help them evacuate in case Mindy breaks and tells her their location. Egan sounded stressed, but there was so much at stake.

I brushed my fingers against the bracelet and stared the falcon shifter down. "Is this a trick?" He'd been outside too, so if the witch had gotten to Mindy, she could've gotten to him as well.

"No, I swear." He lifted a hand. "This is me trying to prove my loyalty to you."

"Where is this place?" Draco asked.

"It's in South Georgia." Ollie gestured to the sky. "Only a couple hours' flight or over a ten-hour car drive."

Egan intertwined our fingers and headed toward the house. "We leave at sunset."

"Okay." Ollie headed into the blue house.

I couldn't shake the feeling that something was off, but Ollie couldn't lie to me while I had the bracelet ... unless the witch had figured out another way to control him superseding the power over the bracelet.

CHAPTER SIXTEEN

W e entered our bedroom in Sadie and Donovan's house, and Egan sat on the bed, putting his head in his hands.

"Hey." I shut the door and kneeled in front of him, placing my elbows on his knees. "We'll find her." I pushed down the annoyance building inside me to keep a level head. For the second time today, I reminded myself that he and Mindy had grown up together. It was normal that he'd be upset.

"That's not what this is about." Egan rubbed a hand down his face and dropped his hands on top of me. "Not only are you in danger, but our entire thunder is too. I won't lie; I don't want Mindy hurt, but she keeps putting people at risk. She should've known better than to run off like that."

"Of course you don't want her hurt. Neither do I." Although I wouldn't object to smacking her around some more, but I'd gotten a solid punch in that should've made my point with her. If not, I could always punch her again. I'd come to terms that I'd be stuck with her since we were like family. "We'll get through this." We didn't have any other option.

He placed his hands on my waist and picked me up so I straddled him. My legs could barely wrap around him, that was how muscular he was.

Gently, he cupped my cheek. "If anything were to happen to you, I don't know what I'd do. Being my mate has already put you in harm's way twice within two months. The first time with your roommate, and the second with Mindy."

His guilt ran clearly between us. It infuriated me that he blamed himself. "This is not your fault. You never asked for that to happen, and I wouldn't change what we have for the world. Would you?"

His face softened as he stared deep into my eyes. "No. I could never give you up, even if that makes me extremely selfish."

I kissed him and poured all my love for him into our bond, wanting him to feel the sincerity of my words. *I've never been this happy, and there are no take-backs.* The truth of my words sank into him. The only time I'd come close to being this happy was that day at the beach with the boy so many years ago, but even that paled in comparison.

His tongue slipped inside my mouth as his hand circled my neck. *The thought of us ever being apart terrifies me.*

Good. I breathed in his citrus scent as his fingers dug into my hip, turning me on. *There's no way I'd let you leave.*

A groan escaped him, and I ground against him. I would never get enough of him. His tongue stroked mine, feeling like velvet and turning me into mush in his arms.

Sadie and the others were still outside talking, leaving us alone in the house for once. I hadn't planned on taking advantage of the time, but now it was the only thing on my mind.

I pulled away from his mouth and kissed down his neck. When I got to the spot where I could feel his pulse against my tongue, I bit ever so gently.

He shook underneath me and purred in satisfaction. He turned his neck, giving me more access.

Leaning back, I lifted his shirt and pulled it over his head. I tossed it over my shoulder and placed my palms on his pecs. His muscles constricted underneath them as his hands grabbed my ass, pushing me harder against him.

Even through our clothing, the friction had started to build. My teeth scratched across his skin, and Egan rolled me onto my back. My body was trapped under his as his mouth peppered kisses toward my chest. He lifted my shirt and unfastened my bra, then placed his lips on my nipple.

My body arched, needing more of his touch, of his body, of everything. I unbuttoned his jeans and slid my hand inside his boxers. I ran my hand along him.

Dammit, Jade. You're driving me crazy. I was going to take it slow. He undressed me, dragging my panties off. His hand slid between my legs as his other one pushed his pants and boxers down.

Next time, I panted without any shame.

He grabbed my waist and tugged me so my ass was right on the edge of the bed. *Fine.* He moved between my legs and thrust inside me.

This time, he wasn't gentle at all, and I loved it. I moaned loudly as he clutched my ankle, lifting my legs higher so he thrust even deeper. His other hand slipped between my legs and rubbed.

Each movement went deeper than the last, slamming into the perfect spot. My body was already primed for him.

His fingers rubbed harder as he increased his pace. I clutched the sheets.

My breath caught as the pleasure built, and soon Egan and I were falling over the edge. He jerked as he finished inside me, and my body quivered from all of the sensations. He lay beside me and pulled me into his naked, sweaty arms.

There was no place I'd rather be.

My eyes grew heavy from the weight of everything that had happened today, and I dozed off.

I WOKE up alone in bed. The void hit me, and I glanced around the room. I was in the center of the bed, completely covered. *Egan?*

Hey, I'm downstairs. He linked. *I'm sorry, I didn't mean to stay down here so long. Draco knocked a little while ago and wanted to talk before leaving.*

You should've woken me. I climbed out of bed and snatched my clothes from the floor. I quickly dressed to join whatever conversation they were having. The room was already darkening, telling me it was later than I'd expected. It was close to sunset, so we'd be heading out soon.

I'm sorry. You were sleeping so good, and after the rough start, I thought a little rest would help with the long night ahead.

I couldn't get too upset at that logic. *I'm on my way.*

I opened the door and heard Draco's voice as clearly as if I were in the same room as him. I hurried down the stairs.

"I understand that her bracelet can control Ollie, but we can't go in there blind," Draco said.

"If you drive, we can go with you," Sadie suggested.

Egan sighed. "We can't chance that timeline. It'll take five times as long. Our thunder could be compromised in that time."

"Speaking of which, did you let them know what's going on?" Donovan asked.

When I stepped into the kitchen, Egan turned to me and patted his lap. He answered the others, his eyes staying on me, "Yes, and they're preparing in case they have to evacuate."

Everyone except Ollie was in the kitchen, sitting around the table, and there wasn't a vacant chair. I guessed that was why he'd gestured for me to come to him, and I'd take any opportunity to be close to him.

"What's the plan? There's no telling if or when Mindy could break. We wouldn't know until the witch attacked." I didn't know how big the thunder was, but if they'd been hiding for centuries, I assumed it was a decent size despite their dwindling numbers. I sat in his lap, and he wrapped his arms around me.

"Hopefully, she can hold out for a day. If we can't locate her, then we relocate the thunder and hope no one else gets taken. There's only a handful of people who know where all the other thunders are located, so the majority of the race should be safe. It's just our thunder at risk."

"All it takes is the witch finding one person who can lead her to them all." Draco pinched the bridge of his nose. "We might need reinforcements."

"Not for this." Egan shook his head. "The rest of your family should stay close unless we know, without a doubt, we're at risk."

Lillith lifted a brow. "There is absolutely no question where your thunder will go. You guys will come and stay in the mountains."

152 JEN L. GREY

Egan tensed. "I'd hate to put your family out like that again."

"Stop it." Sadie pointed a finger at him. "You helped us, so of course Titan's pack will make room for you."

"And we have a huge-ass mansion with plenty of bedrooms that can hold at least twenty, if not more," Lillith added.

"Including all the woods in between," Katherine piped in.

"Hell, I'm down just for Julie's cooking. Katherine, your mom can cook. I miss it." Roxy rubbed her stomach.

Axel frowned. "She even talks about it during sex."

"Dude, really?" Donovan plugged his ears. "I don't want to know that kind of stuff. You used to be more couth until you mated with Roxy."

Roxy waved her hand. "Oh, please. That's bullshit, and you know it."

Donovan growled, "Okay, maybe a stretch, but not this bad."

Moments like these made it seem like the world wasn't so bad. I enjoyed listening to their back and forth.

A knock at the door interrupted the moment.

"I wonder who that could be?" Roxy deadpanned.

Donovan glowered at her.

"I'll go get it. Ollie is uncomfortable enough as it is without us making him stay out there longer than necessary." Katherine chuckled as she stood and hurried to the front door.

"Hey, at least he knocks." I gestured to Roxy. "You should be thankful for that."

"True. Mindy busted in like she owned the joint." Roxy pursed her lips.

"Just remember that the nest and Mom's pack is where

you're going if needed," Sadie said discreetly to Egan as the front door opened. "You did so much for us, and we want to return the favor. Mom said she'll be pissed if you go somewhere else."

Why can't we bring them here? They were all on the same page, so I had to be missing something.

Because the nest and Sadie's mom's pack is still hidden compared to here. Everyone pretty much knows about this place, but only a handful of people know where Cassius and Titan live. We'd be safer there.

Ollie entered the kitchen with a gray bag on his shoulder, Katherine following right behind. From the doorway, he glanced at everyone sitting around the table. "Are you guys ready? I told the witch, Trixie, we'd get there around midnight. Her magic is strongest then, apparently."

"Sounds like a plan." As long as Trixie could block Vera from finding Egan or me, that was all that mattered. I only hoped she could locate Mindy too, but I had a feeling that was a stretch.

"Let's get going then," he said, rocking on his feet.

Egan huffed as I stood. There was no point in avoiding the inevitable.

"Would one of you mind carrying my bag for me?" He winced. "It's impossible for me to do it in my falcon form."

"Sure, I can." I took the bag and turned to Egan. "We should pack some things too." I didn't want to be stuck in my birthday suit down there.

"Already did." Egan gestured to a black bag on the floor by the door. "Draco put his stuff in there too."

"Well, okay then." I had to get used to bringing a backup outfit. I'd never had to worry about it before, but if I didn't get my head on straight, I'd get stuck in a very uncomfortable situation.

Egan, Ollie, and I headed toward the back door.

"Call us if you need anything," Sadie said, her forehead creasing.

The four of us went into the woods behind the house and stripped down to shift. This was only my second time, and my heart pounded. What if I couldn't do it again?

I closed my eyes, seeking the flames inside. Thankfully, they blazed in response to my nonverbal request. My dragon appeared, and all of my anxiety faded.

My body expanded as my wings ripped from my back. My vision became clearer, and the trees appeared to become smaller as my larger size took over. I stepped into the opening between the woods and Sadie's home and found Draco and Egan waiting for me.

Oh, snap, I almost forgot. I spun around and grabbed Ollie's bag with a talon. A *kakking* caught my attention as Ollie took to the sky.

It was time to go.

Draco took off, leaving Egan and me behind.

You ready? Egan asked.

Yes. My wings moved on their own. My beast instinctively knew how to take over. My body lifted skyward, and Egan stayed right next to me. Within minutes, we were flying high.

I glanced down, watching the world grow smaller underneath me. I'd always thought flying in an airplane was amazing, but nothing compared to this. The wind blew under my wings, and the cool night sky caressed my skin. I'd never experienced anything like this before.

Egan chuckled. *You're purring.*

Being here like this, with you by my side, I feel completely content. I probably sounded like an ass with all the shit we were going through.

No, I understand. Having you here next to me fulfills me in a way I didn't know I was lacking. It's okay to be content despite bad things happening. Otherwise, no one would ever be happy. He flew closer to me reassuringly.

He was right. If we let the bad outweigh the good, there would be no smiles or laughter. Just because I was enjoying the moment didn't mean I wasn't worried about what happened next. I would enjoy the next few hours.

We were flying high and covering ground quickly. When the moon began to peak, Ollie started his descent.

As we prepared to land, I realized we were in a thick section of woods. The location was more remote than Sadie's pack house.

We followed Ollie to a small cottage in the center of a flattened area. The house was fifty miles away from anything. A faint light flickered in a window, and when we were several hundred yards away, a thin, short, older lady came into view. Her eyes were locked on me, and an evil smile crossed her face. She lifted her hand, and light reflected off her face. Something dark permeated from deep within her.

Maybe Draco had been right. Ollie could have led us straight into a trap.

CHAPTER SEVENTEEN

I hated asking, but the witch made my skin crawl. We were only about a hundred yards away from her and descending quickly. With every inch I got closer to her, my internal warning clamored louder. *Should we go back?*

We don't have much of a choice. Egan sounded resolved and not as panicked as me. *Shifters generally feel uncomfortable around witches and their magic. The witches use the magic of the nature that we're in touch with. Since we can feel the disturbance that they create, it kind of goes against our very nature. But stay close to Draco and me in case something happens. I don't sense anyone else around, so I think we're okay.*

My dragon surged forward, tapping into our surroundings. I didn't detect any worrisome smells or sounds, confirming what Egan had said. I had to get used to being part animal since the extra-sensitive senses came in handy.

We landed, and the light illuminating her face dimmed as she stepped toward us. Her charcoal eyes took in our dragon forms, and she smirked. "I never thought I'd see one dragon in my lifetime, yet here three of you stand. Your race has hidden for so long, we all thought you'd gone extinct here on Earth."

She gestured to the woods behind us, and a few wisps of her silver hair fell from the bun teetering on top of her head. "Please, shift back into human form so we can speak."

Some of my anxiety calmed since she didn't seem so creepy now.

Egan stepped backward to the woods, not willing to turn his back on the witch. *Change right next to me,* he commanded, which annoyed me.

Fine, I will this time. But next time, why don't you ask? Maybe he was being protective, but that didn't mean he could treat me like that. I demanded respect, even when it was hard to give.

Now's not the time. Egan jerked his head toward the woods. *I'm trying to keep you safe, so be rational.*

The worst thing he could have done was tell me to be rational; every fiber of my being wanted to do the complete opposite out of spite. This new protective alpha male attitude better change fast. I did what any woman would have done to prove something to herself. I dropped Ollie's bag next to some trees so he could shift back without me having to see his dangly bits and stomped off to a section of woods farther away from Egan.

Of course, I hadn't thought that through, and the ground shook under each pounding footstep. At least, that drove the point home.

Where are you going? he asked in exasperation.

Away from you. I lifted my head high.

Good luck with that, Egan said with a chuckle.

Oh, I'd show him funny, but then I paused. Dammit, he had my clothes. I needed to change next to him, and it infuriated me. I had a problem doing what someone told me to.

Mustering up some dignity, I straightened my back and folded my wings to appear more rigid. I marched over to Egan and took the bag off the forest floor. If the situation hadn't been dire, I would've run off with them, but I had to be somewhat mature.

Even in dragon form, I could see Egan's shit-eating smile as he watched me head to the area he wanted me to change in. If I could have flipped him off, I would've.

I walked behind a section of trees and closed my eyes, pushing away all of the negativity. This was only my second shift back to human, so I wanted to concentrate. Like the previous time, my dragon released its hold on me without much of a struggle. My body began to change back to human just as Egan joined me.

Back in human form, I took my clothes from the bag and changed, ignoring my now naked mate beside me as he put on his jeans. I was still unhappy with him.

As I placed the bracelet in my pocket and moved to walk past him, he wrapped an arm around me and pulled me toward his naked chest. Thankfully, he had his jeans back on or things might have gotten out of hand.

I'm sorry for treating you like that. The witch is making me nervous, and I needed you next to me to keep me from losing my mind. He kissed me and let me go.

Unfortunately, my traitorous heart had already forgiven him. I wanted to stay upset a little longer, but that wasn't happening. *I understand, but no more macho asshole. Okay?*

He slipped his shirt on, his stomach muscles bunching, and a bit of drool collected in the corner of my mouth. He was so damn hot and all mine, the combination impossibly appealing.

Picking up the bag, he held my hand as we moved toward the witch. *I promise.*

When we stepped out of the woods, he released his hold on me. *Give me one second.*

He took off toward where Draco had gone and tossed the bag behind the large tree where the warrior dragon was waiting. In a flash, Egan was beside me again.

We returned to the witch and found Ollie standing next to her, waiting on us.

Needing to make sure I could still control Ollie, I fingered the bracelet in my pocket and spoke low so only Egan and Draco could hear. "Hug the witch and kiss her cheek."

Immediately, Ollie turned to the witch, pulled her into a tight embrace, and kissed her cheek.

The older lady's eyes widened, and she jerked away from him, wiping the slobber from her face. "What—"

I bit the inside of my cheek to stop myself from bursting into laughter.

Ollie swallowed loudly as he glared at me. "Trixie, these are the fated mate dragons I told you about. The witch that controlled me got her blood and has been using it to locate Jade."

"Yes, blood is very powerful in all types of magic. It is nice to meet you, Jade, even though it's not under the best of circumstances." Trixie held her hand out to me.

"I appreciate you helping us." I couldn't say it was nice to meet her, because it wasn't. I wished the circumstances had been different and I hadn't needed to meet her at all. But I forced myself to shake her hand.

The witch's grip took me by surprise. She was older, close to seventy, but her grip was strong. I didn't know what I'd been expecting, but it definitely wasn't that.

"And I'm Egan." My mate shook her hand, his face expressionless.

"I expected you two, but who is the other dragon?" Trixie asked as she looked around Egan to Draco.

"Another dragon joined us when the witch started giving us problems. She might be holding a female dragon from our thunder captive, and we're hoping you can locate her," Egan explained.

"I can try, but no promises. A witch that can spell something to control another person is very strong. Not many can do that, and I'm sure she made it impossible to track down the female dragon even with a personal item of hers."

"But if you could try—" Ollie started.

"Of course I will, boy." She patted his arm. "I just hate I can't do more." She faced me. "Ollie told me about that bracelet you grabbed. May I see it?"

Yeah, that wasn't happening. I didn't know this woman, and I wouldn't hand over the one thing keeping Ollie loyal to us. "Not right now."

Her eyebrows lifted, and she opened her mouth to respond, but Draco joined us with the bag, stepping beside me.

I felt sandwiched between the two towering men.

"The moon is high, and Ollie said something about you needing to use your magic at its peak," Egan interjected, changing the subject.

"Yes, that's true." The witch licked her lips and held out her hand to me, palm facing up. "Please put your hand on mine and let me see if I can sense what's going on."

We'd just told her what was going on, but I'd humor her if it got her to help me. I did as she asked, and her hand warmed mine as something passed from her into me. I instinctively closed my eyes, not wanting to watch as everyone stared at me.

The warmth connected with my blood. I guessed it

made sense since blood made magic the most powerful. As it threaded inside me, though, it felt cold and uncomfortable.

Is something wrong? Egan asked with concern. *I'm getting a weird emotion from you.*

I had no clue what I was feeling. *I don't think so. I can feel her magic, and it's cold.*

That's because your blood runs hot now with your dragon. Anything outside our norm feels cold. But if you feel any pain or like someone is attacking your mind, let me know.

"Yes," Trixie murmured. "I can feel her all over you. She has a spell on you that informs her where you are." Her hand tensed on mine.

I blinked and found myself staring into the witch's eyes. They were no longer charcoal. Instead, they were a vivid silver that glowed as brightly as the moon and her hair.

"Can you do something?" It freaked me out that Vera became alerted whenever I went somewhere. I'd thought she'd been locating me at certain points in time. I almost felt like my aunt was watching me again.

"Maybe." Her hand gripped mine harder, and more power trickled into me.

My dragon roared and surfaced into my mind. She didn't like what I was allowing to happen, and she wanted me to stop it.

I wasn't sure how to make her understand, and the flames flicked within me like my blood was going to war with the witch.

Something sparked as my dragon attacked the foreign magic. The cold crashed against the increasing temperature. I groaned as my knees buckled, and Egan's comforting arm wrapped around my waist, bearing my weight.

Babe, what's going on? he asked, alarmed.

Her magic just feels foreign. I had no clue what Trixie was doing, but my dragon did.

"What are you doing to her?" Draco asked warningly.

"I'm burning off the magic the other witch linked with her blood." She pushed even more magic inside me.

I sagged against Egan as my internal war intensified. The oddest sensations of hot and cold mixed as the two parts collided.

"Just a little longer," Trixie gasped.

Her eyes were now a blinding, piercing white. I shut my eyes again to find the strength to hold on.

Egan's worry slammed into me. *Maybe we should tell her to stop.*

No. If this was the key to preventing Vera from tracking us, I'd gladly endure it. I only had to hold on long enough for Trixie to finish.

But if your dragon—

The witch released me and staggered away. Her chest heaved, proving she'd struggled as hard as I had.

"Are you okay?" Ollie asked the older lady, touching her shoulder to steady her.

"Give me a moment, and I will be." She lifted her head toward the moon, basking in its light. Her hands shook as she wrapped her arms around her body.

The flames inside me roared, trying to keep the cold at bay until the cold tendrils vanished.

Is your dragon calming? Egan kept a firm hold on me, afraid I might fall.

Yeah, she is. Whatever the witch did has either settled or burned off. I didn't know another way to describe it.

Draco stepped closer, his body coiled, ready to attack.

Everyone was on edge, but I had a feeling until we relocated the thunder or found Mindy, we'd remain this way.

Trixie inhaled sharply and lowered her head to look at me. "You're really strong. I almost couldn't finish."

As strength returned to my body, I moved away from Egan to carry my own weight. I loved that I could count on Egan, but I had to stand on my own two feet.

His hand stayed firmly around me. *Don't rush it.*

I'm not. I'm good, I promise.

When he didn't smell a lie, he released his hold while the corners of his mouth still dipped downward. He hated that I had to endure all this.

"Did it work?" If I'd gone through all of that for nothing, I'd be awfully pissy.

"Yes, child. You're free from the witch's spell." More of Trixie's hair had fallen out of her bun during the intense connection we'd shared.

"What about the female dragon?" Ollie asked. "Can you find her?"

"Yes, that won't take nearly as much power." She nodded and pulled on her long brown dress. "But I need something of hers."

"How about hair?" Draco pulled a hairbrush from our shared bag. "We took this from her room."

"That will work perfectly." She took the brush and kneeled on the ground. She reached into her pocket and pulled out a knife and a paper map.

Her outfit hadn't impressed me, but now that I realized it was a dress with pockets, I kind of wanted one of my own.

The metallic scent of blood pulled me back to the moment, and I realized the witch had cut her palm.

She'd laid the map flat against the ground with the

brush sitting on top. She rocked as she chanted, "*Locum tuum revelare.*"

After repeating the words three more times, she placed her hand over the brush and map and let several large blood drops fall on both items.

The wind picked up, and thunder crashed despite the cloudless night. Then the ground shook, and Trixie flew backward several feet.

Lightning hit the map as another bolt raced toward us.

CHAPTER EIGHTEEN

D raco lunged, knocking Egan and me to the ground as the lightning barreled over our heads.

If I'd felt sandwiched between the two men earlier, I'd been grossly exaggerating. My front lay flat against Egan with Draco draped over my back. Smushed between their bodies, I struggled to breathe.

The quaking earth rattled us, and their bodies jostled me, making my teeth clatter together. Vera was pissed and letting everyone know. And hell, she probably wanted to instill some fear in us.

I was thinking we were goners until the thunder tapered off and the world stilled. The silence was almost deafening after the chaos.

Neither Draco nor Egan moved—like they were waiting for the mayhem to start again.

I can't breathe. I squirmed, trying to get up, but I could barely move an inch. My head spun, warning me I wasn't getting enough oxygen. Before now, I hadn't thought it was possible to get too close to Egan. But boy, was I wrong.

"We're good," Ollie said, his voice sounding farther

away. He had to be checking on Trixie. "Whatever that was is gone for now."

Draco moved, digging his side into my back and pushing me harder into Egan. My lungs screamed for air. After another second, his weight disappeared as he kneeled beside us.

I lifted my head and inhaled sharply, giving my body a moment to recover.

"Dammit," Draco growled.

I jumped to my feet. I pushed away any leftover discomfort and followed his gaze.

The map and hairbrush had disintegrated.

"Trixie." Ollie squatted beside her, gently patting her face.

If I hadn't heard her strong heartbeat, I would've thought she was dead.

A cold breeze churned, icy tendrils wrapping around us. Whatever clung to my skin was bone-chilling and laced with a deep, dark warning.

Draco turned slowly, surveying the area. "The witch is taunting us."

She couldn't have arrived here this fast, or I hoped not. But we had a more imminent threat to worry about—Trixie could be severely injured. I wasn't sure what magic was capable of and whether someone could be harmed from this far away.

Rushing over to Trixie and Ollie, I scanned the witch for any injuries. I couldn't see any, which made me worry more. Internal injuries were often more serious. I brushed her hair from her face, ignoring the breeze growing stronger. "Can we help?"

"Not really," Egan answered, hovering next to me. "She'll have to wake on her own."

"It's getting cold out here." We didn't have time to wait. Between the chill in the air and the threat of another storm, we needed to move her somewhere safe or wake her up so she could protect herself.

Doing the only thing I could think of, I bent at the waist and slapped her in the face a lot harder than Ollie had.

"Hey!" Ollie exclaimed. "Be careful with her. She's old."

Trixie's eyes fluttered. "I heard that, *boy*."

He winced. "I'm sorry. It's just—"

"You don't ever call a woman old, even if it is true," she scolded and opened her eyes.

"Yes, ma'am." Ollie nodded. "I didn't mean—"

"It's fine." Trixie sat up and rubbed her hands along her arms. "You've pissed off someone stronger than I've ever seen. Magic like that ..." She trailed off and shuddered.

She couldn't stop there. "What do you mean?"

"Old magic is much stronger than the kind you find today, but the strength of her power isn't possible."

"Not possible?" Egan's forehead lined with confusion.

"Strong witches still exist in the world but not nearly as strong as what they used to be." Trixie gazed at the stars. "As with most things, our bloodline has become more diluted, taking some of our power away. The power she has means she's pure-blooded or really old."

"Do witches live a long time?" Ollie asked, curiosity getting the better of him.

"We have a normal human lifespan, unlike shifters, which makes me think she's the purest witch I've ever encountered." She gestured to the charred ground. "I couldn't do something like that."

"I'm assuming there's no way to find Mindy." Draco gazed at where she'd pointed.

"So Mindy must be the girl I was trying to locate," Trixie said.

"Yes, it is," Egan said as he placed a hand protectively around my waist.

I stepped into his side, wanting to be closer.

The witch gestured to the ashes of the map and hairbrush. "There's no way now, and honestly, I wouldn't be thrilled about trying again. She tried connecting with my magic, but I held her off, barely. I'm not sure I could fight her off again."

Egan's face fell. "We don't want you to get hurt. You've done more than enough." *I'll need to help relocate the thunder and inform Mindy's parents that we can't find her.*

You? If he thought that would fly over well with me, he was dead wrong. *Nope. We.*

But if Mindy gives up the thunder's location, you could be in harm's way.

I faced him, allowing my rage to surge between us. *Let me be clear. We are partners and equals, which means we stick together. If you don't stop treating me like I'm delicate, we're going to have a serious problem.*

Feeling the gravity of my words, he frowned. *It's not that I think you're delicate or weak, I just don't want anything bad happening to you. I couldn't live with myself if you got hurt or worse.*

And you think I could live with you getting hurt? Don't be an egotistical, selfish prick. If you can put yourself at risk, so can I. I turned my back on him and closed our connection. He would only continue to rationalize why he was acting that way, and I wasn't interested.

I focused back on Trixie as the wind howled. "We need to get you inside."

"I'm fine." Trixie patted Ollie's hand. "You need to go.

That's the only way this will calm down. She's making sure I don't attempt the spell again."

Draco glanced at Egan. "I don't sense anyone physically here, and the longer we stay, the greater the risk to your thunder. We should go now."

"All right." Egan sighed and brushed against our connection.

Nope, I refused to let him try to talk me out of going with him. He'd only piss me off more and make me more determined to prove myself by likely doing something stupid. For my sanity and his, he best back the hell off.

"Thank you for everything," I said to Trixie then arched an eyebrow at Egan. "I'm going to change." I grabbed the bag and rushed toward the woods, ready to strip down and shift into my dragon. I hated wasting time to change, but I refused to meet Egan's parents in the nude. I didn't give a damn if they were shifters.

The three guys followed closely behind me, and Egan said, "Ollie, you need to go back to the pack house and let them know what happened. Vera may attack them since she can't locate us anymore. They need to prepare with as many capable hands as possible."

"Got it," Ollie agreed. "I'll head straight there."

I stopped and faced them. "Maybe I should—" I reached for the bracelet in my pocket.

"Look, I get you don't trust me, but give me a chance to earn it." Ollie frowned. "We both want the witch to die."

He was right. I hadn't given him a chance, and I knew what it felt like not to be given a second chance. "Fine. Don't make me regret it."

He headed off into the woods to shift with Draco following close behind.

I hid behind some trees and undressed, putting my

clothes and bracelet in the bag. My dragon surged forward, the flames licking my mind. With little effort, and more quickly, my body began to change. She and I were connecting and working together as one. As I turned fully beast, Egan joined me. He pulled out his cell phone from the bag and typed a message.

I opened the connection between us. *Are you texting your parents?* I didn't know why, but I hadn't even considered messaging them to let them know how dire the situation was. In my mind, we had to race there to let them know what we'd discovered.

Yeah, and Sadie. I want them to know what's going on and that Ollie is heading back to them. If he doesn't show up, we need to know.

I wasn't concerned about Ollie since he'd proved he was still under the control of the bracelet. He couldn't hear my words earlier, and I doubted he would've willingly kissed or hugged the witch. My shoulders shook with laughter, remembering her expression. Nonetheless, it didn't hurt to have some reassurance.

Done with his phone, he tossed it and his clothes into the bag, and soon, his huge dragon form stood right beside me.

We returned to the clearing and found only Draco waiting. The witch was gone, and Ollie was halfway into the sky, flying north.

The wind had calmed. Either the witch had focused elsewhere, or she was waiting for us to take to the air before attacking again. Neither option was ideal.

Egan linked as his wings flapped. *Keep an eye out.*

I'd planned on it, I bit back as I ascended.

The entire way into the sky, I had to keep reminding myself to breathe. I kept holding my breath as if I could hear an attack coming better, but it only made my head loopy. If the witch attacked, I needed to have a clear mind.

When we reached a high enough elevation in the cloudless sky so humans couldn't see us, my heart steadied. We'd already warded off several attacks, so maybe the rest of the trip would be smooth sailing.

A girl could hope.

The guys flanked me as we flew back toward Tennessee, and I realized I was clueless about where we were heading. *How long until we get there?*

Only a couple of hours. Our thunder is an hour north of Knoxville, in the mountains near Gatlinburg.

I'd expected them to be halfway across the world, not so close to Kortright University. Maybe it was the slight accent he and Draco had that had given me the impression.

The moon descended during our flight. Every mile we traveled made my dragon side feel even more antsy. I wasn't sure what was going on, but she was on edge.

We're only thirty minutes away. Egan linked, almost startling me.

For the past several hours, we'd flown in silence. *Is there anything I should know before we arrive?*

I don't think so. He flew closer to me, his golden eyes locking on mine.

How many are in your thunder? Are they okay with Draco coming? Are there any other ex-girlfriends or betrotheds I should know about? More questions almost tumbled from my lips, but I held them back. Those were more than enough for now. The problem was there was no telling what I was walking into, and the unknown unsettled me.

Egan chuckled. *I should've known you'd have a ton of questions. Our thunder is around two hundred but dwin-*

dling. There hasn't been a new birth since me. My father was the last dragon allowed to find his fated mate before me.

How is that possible? I thought dragons had been in hiding for several centuries.

He looked forward as we approached a large mountain. *Dragons can live for hundreds of years. My parents had me when they were in their sixties. They weren't in a hurry to start a family until after my grandfather died.*

Wait ... *How old are you?*

Don't worry, I'm only twenty-two years old. Dragons age like humans until they reach their mid-twenties.

My relief caught me by surprise. Dating a forty-year-old man who looked twenty would've bothered me. *Thank God. But that means your parents are in their eighties.*

But they look like they're in their mid to late thirties. So, we won't have to take care of them any time soon. He winked.

I stared at him in awe. Dragons could wink!

And they know Draco is coming. In fact, Dad expected him to come. He fell silent.

I realized ... *Is there a reason you're dodging the ex-girl-friends question?*

Not at all. I just have nothing to share on that front. You are my first in all ways, Jade, he said gently.

All of my earlier anger against him dissipated. How the hell could I stay mad at him after he'd said something like that? *I had a horrible first kiss, but everything else is the same about you.*

Annoyance flared inside him. *You kissed other guys?*

Only one, and it was horrible. My stomach revolted at the memory of all of the drool. *I've never done anything else with anyone and definitely never felt this way for anyone.*

Good, he rasped. *I'd hate to have to kill a human.*

A chuckle bubbled inside me right before raw panic slammed into me. The urge to turn around grew so strong it stole my breath. *We need to turn around. Something's wrong.*

Dammit, I forgot about this. Egan sounded tense. *Jade, it's just the barrier. We use magic to stay hidden, and the barrier repels anything that isn't part of our thunder.*

But I am. Were they rejecting me?

After you've passed through the barrier once, this won't happen again. I need you to stay strong and trust me.

That was a huge ask, but I knew what I had to do. I clutched onto my dragon tightly, and we resolved to push through this obstacle.

Egan descended, and Draco and I followed suit. Draco didn't seem to have any issues passing through the barrier.

Why isn't he struggling? Draco wasn't part of his thunder either, so he should have been struggling too.

The same magic protects all the thunders. Once you're recognized by a barrier, your signature is known by all.

We were so close to the mountain that I could make out the leaves on the trees. Each wing flap increased my urge to flee. Right when I thought we were going to land, I ran into resistance and plummeted.

CHAPTER NINETEEN

My wings flapped, keeping me elevated, but everything inside screamed that I was dropping. My dragon surged forward in a panic, and I focused on the fact that everything was fine. We were only a couple hundred yards from landing on the mountain.

Just a little bit longer, Egan assured me.

As we reached the treetops, the surrounding air churned and spun. A sphere-shaped vortex pulsed before me, and the land blurred.

All of the colors mixed, and the sensation of falling hit me harder.

Egan! I cried. I couldn't make anything out.

Frustration laced his words as he said, *It's almost over. Hold on. I'm right here.*

His presence was the only thing keeping me together. If it hadn't been for him, I'd have already given up.

Disoriented, I continued my steady trek forward. We should have been landing. We'd been so close seconds ago.

I tensed, bracing for impact, but the churning stopped,

and the overwhelming sensation of falling dissolved. Colors came back into focus as the mountain view vanished.

I couldn't believe my eyes.

A large cave surrounded by the woods appeared. The opening faced the sky, surrounded by green moss covering the rocks, and was large enough for us to enter in our beast forms one at a time.

What is that? I asked Egan, thankful that the intense feelings had disappeared. They'd been so fierce that I wasn't sure how I'd fought through them. They had vanished just in time because I wasn't sure how much longer I could have ignored the urge to turn away.

The entrance to the thunder. Egan descended with Draco and me right behind him.

Animals scurried loudly in the woods as we approached the opening. *Why is it so much louder here?*

No one travels through here because we rarely leave, and no outsider has ever made it through the spell. The animals aren't scared like they are outside of here. They've been protected the same way we have.

That was interesting. This was what our world would sound like if fear didn't exist.

Egan expertly fit through the opening, and Draco held back, allowing me to go next.

There was no telling what waited inside, but I couldn't let my trepidation hold me back. This was my new life, and coming here to help them evacuate was the way I needed to help my thunder and Egan's parents. I had to be strong, especially since Egan wasn't thrilled about me tagging along.

My dragon took more control, wanting to navigate a little while longer. I was more than happy to oblige. Having her mostly in control wasn't as worrisome as it had been at the beginning.

She took root in my mind and flitted us through the opening. Her excitement was contagious. Her meeting the thunder was the next most important thing to bonding with Egan.

Once inside the cave, I couldn't believe my eyes. I'd expected to find a dark, cold hole, but the cave was the opening to a huge valley at least a hundred miles wide. Next, I spotted an area comprising a village of large log cabins. A huge river ran through the outer section of rolling grassy hills. Next to the river lay vast farmland where all types of crops grew along with pastures containing cows and pigs.

I looked over my shoulder as Draco entered. The hole was the only way in or out but also seemed to be the way for the sun to shine into the valley.

I'd never seen anything so beautiful in my entire life. *I was not expecting this.*

Egan's happiness flowed into me. He faced me as he replied, *I'm glad you approve, and I wish we weren't rushing everyone to leave. I really wanted to share my childhood home with you.*

Maybe you can. Hopefully, Mindy would surprise us and refuse to give up the thunder's location. We had our doubts about her after she'd hidden instead of fighting alongside us, but maybe when she was forced to stand and fight, she would. I prayed, for all our sakes, that we were just being extremely cautious.

I hope so, but we can't chance our entire thunder on that. Egan headed toward the cabins.

There had to be over one hundred houses. A few people

stood outside, looking directly at us, with at least fifty bags at their feet.

Egan flew past them and headed to the house in the center. People were focused on me and Draco, their faces lined with concern.

Oh, great. We were outsiders, and they weren't thrilled with us invading their thunder. I knew those looks all too well. That was how everyone in my aunt's entire neighborhood and the school I'd attended had treated me. Anyone outside their clique was treated with mistrust.

In other words—stranger danger. That concept mostly applied to little kids and held merit, but not when adults treated a child with prejudice. I shuddered at the memories. *That's a warm welcome.*

It's more at Draco than you. They know I'm mated and you're part of this thunder. They'll treat you like one of us; they just need to get to know you first.

He was probably right. My negativity stemmed from childhood baggage. What were they supposed to do, run up and throw their human arms around me? They probably couldn't due to my huge-ass frame anyway, and then I'd be freaked out because they'd touched me. These people couldn't win in my mind, and I worked to turn my perspective around. Combine that with the imminent threat of an attack, and of course, they were coming off as indifferent.

As we drew closer to the center house, I realized the doorway was huge. Our dragon forms could easily fit through it.

I guessed that was a perk of living in a thunder. The houses had been made to accommodate our beast forms.

My mate landed, and the door opened, revealing a woman with the same shade of blonde hair as his but pulled back into a long braid. She was an inch shorter than me in human form, which somehow comforted me. I figured I'd be the smallest one in the thunder, but maybe I wouldn't stick out after all.

Her moss-green eyes locked on me, and a smile broke across her face. "You must be Jade." She stepped toward me before stopping. She sighed. "I guess you should shift so we can actually talk and formally meet before welcoming you with open arms." She stepped aside to allow the three of us in.

I stepped into the house, and the sheetrock interior startled me. I'd expected the walls to be made of the same logs as the outside of the house, but it reminded me of all of the homes I'd lived in growing up. The three of us fit comfortably in the foyer. and a human-sized doorway to the right led deeper into the house.

Egan turned to a large door on the left and jerked his head. *Come on. It's the shifting room.*

Of course, they'd have a room designated for that.

The large, empty room took up the entire side of the house, but it was barely big enough for the two of us. Egan moved his wing to drop the bag, and his eyes dimmed as his dragon receded.

Knowing we needed to hurry, my dragon withdrew, and within minutes, I was back in human form.

Egan's eyes perused me.

No. There would be none of that. His mother was right outside the door. I refused for her to hear, see, or smell what he was doing in here. *Get dressed. We have a thunder to save, and we're in your parents' home.*

Not giving him a chance to complain, I snatched my clothes from the bag and dressed.

He sighed in exasperation and retrieved his clothes from the bag. *Fine. You're just tempting is all.*

And to think I once considered you gentlemanly, I teased. I still did, and he was. Our mate sides were just coming out. He always treated everyone with respect.

When he was dressed, he kissed me and laced his fingers with mine. *I would never want to make you feel uncomfortable, especially around my parents. And I'm sorry about earlier. You're right. You deserve to be here with me. It's just my natural instinct is to protect you.*

I struggle with the same thing, so I understand, but you need to realize my aunt made me feel weak, and when I left her, I promised I'd never allow myself to feel that way again. I need you to treat me like I'm your equal in every way. I couldn't hold his earlier behavior against him. My dragon wanted to fiercely protect him the same way.

He cupped my cheek, staring deep into my soul. *You kicked ass against those wolf shifters the other day in your human form. You are a force, and I will never make you feel otherwise again. We will protect each other going forward even if it's hard on us.*

He understood what I needed, proving we were made for each other. He cared about all of me—my mind, body, and soul—the same way I cared for him. *Thank you. I love you.*

I love you too. He tugged me to the door, leaving the bag behind for Draco. *Now let's go help our thunder.*

Words had never sounded so sweet or romantic to me.

Back in the hallway, Egan's dad stood next to his mom. His dad's eyes were the same mesmerizing gold as my mate's, and he had the same striking features. The only difference between them was his father's short cedar hair.

Draco brushed past me into the shifting room, leaving the four of us alone in the entryway.

"Dad. Mom. This is—" Egan started, but his mom cut him off.

"Jade, it's so great to finally meet you." She hugged me and sniffled. "I'm so sorry for what Mindy has put you through and now all this."

"It's not your fault, and everything worked out." I winced. "Okay, 'worked out' might be a stretch. More like fate intervened." Wait, that wasn't much better. My awkwardness reared its ugly head once again. "Not that fate wants you to abandon your home." Oh my God. They were going to hate me.

His mother chuckled warmly. "No, I understand what you mean. And you're right. Fate chose you as his mate. She wouldn't let a jealous dragon shifter get in your way."

It caught me off guard that her presence comforted me almost as much as Egan's did. I'd expected someone prickly, especially knowing how good Egan was. I wasn't good enough for him.

"And it's nice to be introduced to our daughter." His father wrapped his arms around both Egan's mother and me.

The warm greeting shook me. "It's nice to meet you both."

"Please, call us Mom and Dad." His mother beamed.

"Uh ..." I'd just met them. That was a little uncomfortable.

"She means call them Ladon and Kayda." Egan shook his head, his shoulders shaking with quiet laughter. *I'm so sorry about her. She's excited to meet you and can come off a little strong.*

Kayda rubbed a temple. "That was strange asking you to call us that right away. Ladon and Kayda are more than fine."

"Did you travel here without issue?" Ladon asked, changing the topic, much to my relief.

"Yes. Nothing out of the ordinary happened, thankfully." Egan placed an arm around my waist. "How long until everyone is ready to go?"

"Within an hour," Ladon said and looked over my shoulder. "Draco, it's nice to meet you."

"The feeling is mutual." Draco bowed his head formally.

That was odd. *Is that how dragons greet one another?* If so, I'd probably completely offended his parents.

Egan's brows furrowed slightly. *No, I think it's his warrior side coming out.*

"Are you sure about your friends?" Kayda walked through the small doorway, waving for us to follow.

We entered a homey living room that held a couch, a love seat, and a recliner. There wasn't a television but rather a large bookcase filled with books.

"Sadie and Lillith have opened their parents' homes and the woods between their lands to us. We can make do and build a few houses. With our smaller numbers, we could double up some families and get by with what they have available. A few of Titan's pack members moved to Sadie and Donovan's to establish order after everything that went down a few months ago."

"We're so lucky you found such amazing friends." Ladon gestured to the seats in the living room. "Why don't we sit and talk for a minute?"

"Talk?" That was an odd request when we needed to get moving. "Shouldn't we be gathering everyone and figuring out logistics?"

"She's right." Egan pointed to the two bags against the

wall at the base of the stairway. "We can talk later. Right now, we need to help others get situated."

Ladon sat on the loveseat. "We will, but there is something we need to discuss."

"Dad? What's wrong?"

"There's something we haven't told you, honey." Kayda sat next to her husband and took his hand. "We just need a few minutes."

Annoyance wafted off Egan.

Whatever they have to say seems important. I understood where Egan was coming from. This wasn't the best time to sit down and chat, but they seemed like reasonable people. So for them to request this had to mean it needed to be addressed right this moment.

I walked over to the couch and sat in the center. Egan hesitated but followed me over.

Draco stood near the doorway, his shoulders tense.

Whatever they wanted to talk about, Draco knew. The realization didn't sit well with me.

"Son, there's something we've needed to tell you since you were a little boy." Ladon inhaled sharply. "But we needed to wait until you'd found your mate. My father asked me to tell you both at the same time." Something coursed through my blood.

The cold feeling I'd felt with Trixie came back stronger, and my body shook as the magic took hold.

"Jade!" Egan yelled and clutched my arms. "What's wrong?"

CHAPTER TWENTY

The power receded, concerning me more than anything. Vera wasn't concentrating on me anymore, which meant her focus was elsewhere, likely on finding a way in.

"I think the witch tracked us. The coldness coursed through me again, like she was telling me she's here." Trixie had said it worked, but thinking back, she'd never outright said Vera couldn't track us. She'd only implied it. Could she be working with Vera, or was Vera's magic that powerful?

My stomach roiled. If I'd brought her here, that meant I'd essentially sold out the thunder.

Draco started. "But the witch said—"

"I know." He was thinking the same thing as me. "But I don't know what else it could be."

"Maybe she broke Mindy or found a way to control her like Ollie." Egan stood, his body tense. "Either way, it doesn't matter. If she's here, there's no undoing it."

"We need to get you out of here." Draco stepped toward the doorway. "Is there a back way out of here?"

"Yes, but it's not passable." Ladon rubbed his thumb over his bottom lip. "We always use the main entrance."

"Wait." Egan's brows furrowed. "There's a second way out? I never knew that."

"Each thunder only has one person who knows about the second passageway," Draco explained. He rushed to the front of the house. The door opened and closed as the warrior ran outside. He wanted to see what we were up against, giving us time to put a plan into effect.

I still wasn't following. "Why is that?"

"In case of an attack of this magnitude, one person can leave and warn the other thunders. If more than one family knew, it could create a mass exodus, preventing word from getting out that we need help." Kayda hurried over to the bags.

"We need weapons. I'm assuming she didn't come alone to a thunder full of dragons." Ladon walked over to the bookcase and pulled a book out. The house rumbled as a section of the bookcase pivoted outward.

"Why didn't I know about this?" Egan stepped up next to his father and peered inside.

"Because we hoped no one would need to know." He gestured toward the dark room that had guns and ammo lined in a neat row. "Grab a few rifles. Kayda, tell the others what's going on and to bring all the secret stashes of artillery. We need to get ready to fight before they get here."

"On it," Kayda said and raced to the door. "I'll be right back."

"There's no way we can lead all of them to the other exit before the witch arrives." Egan picked up a couple of guns and held them expertly.

"No, that exit is purely for backup. I'm hoping we can

leave out the main one. That's our best bet." Ladon faced me with a smaller gun. "Can you shoot?"

"Yeah, but it's been a minute." A few self-defense classes I'd taken wanted us to be familiar with guns. Not to use but to know how to fight if our attacker had one. They'd taught us to only use them in a worst-case scenario. My instructors had made it clear he didn't approve, but learning about them was necessary to survive.

He gave the handgun to me. "Better than not knowing at all."

"I don't understand." I took the gun. It felt like it weighed a ton, although it had to be a pound, max, in my hand. "Why don't we shift into our dragons and fight?"

"That's likely what the witch wants, and we may be very strong in that form, but we'd also be bigger targets." Ladon selected a black holster that could be tied around an arm or a thigh and handed it to me. "In human form, we can lie low and hide. And sometimes, our human forms can be more lethal, especially when we tap into our dragons to amplify our senses."

I'd never thought of it like that. In beast form, we were huge.

"Maybe you and Mom should go out the back," Egan said as he looked at me. "Dad and I can stay back and fight with the others."

No, he didn't. Maybe he really did have a death wish but wanted me to end him instead of whatever threat we were facing.

I stared him down and let my anger punch each sylla-ble. "Don't you start. Remember the conversation we just had?" I jabbed my finger at the shifting room.

"Son, you can't expect her to leave you. Would you be willing to run and leave her here to fight?" Ladon sighed.

"God, no, but—"

"You better think through your next words." My blood was boiling, ready for a fight. I'd rather it be against the witch, but Egan was about to get the brunt of my anger.

Ladon patted his son's arm. "We have strong mates for a reason."

"You're right." Egan kissed my forehead. "And you can hold your own. I've seen you in action."

"Damn straight I can." And I had a score to settle with my ex-roommate.

The front door swung open and slammed against the wall. Kayda yelled, "We've got a huge problem."

"What is it?" Ladon grabbed the rest of the guns, and we sprinted to the front door.

Draco stood next to her in the entryway.

Kayda's face was as pale as a vampire's, and her eyes had darkened to hunter green. The acidic smell of fear blew off her. "The witch brought harpies."

"Harpies?" Ladon's mouth dropped. "But they're from Fae."

"I told you the fae king warned me they were still looking for us." Egan stepped protectively next to me. "Maybe the witch is connected to them. It would explain how strong she is."

"Fae as in Sadie's dad and aunt's realm?" That was still a foreign concept to me. Another dimension sounded straight out of a science fiction novel.

"Yes." Egan frowned. "We hid because they were hunting us down centuries ago."

"Are the others getting their weapons?" Ladon asked as he handed two guns to Draco.

"They're getting them now." Kayda pushed past us, grabbed the two bags, and threw one over each shoulder.

"We need to get a move on. At least a hundred harpies are heading this way."

"We need to shoot them. The more we take out before they get within fighting range, the better our chances that more of us will come out of this alive." Draco opened the door and left first.

As the rest of us stepped outside, he stood with his gun pointed at the cave opening, covering us, and I could not believe what I saw. At the word 'harpy,' I'd had no clue what to expect, but it certainly wasn't that.

A swarm headed straight toward us. I tapped into my dragon, and the women came into full view—or they looked like women. They were equal parts human and animal. The top half was completely naked and all human. They each had a long torso, two arms, and large, voluptuous breasts. As if that wasn't striking enough, their cruel, weathered faces and deep-set coal eyes made them truly frightful. Their hair was greasy and tangled, and blood crusted their dry, peeling lips. From the torso down, they looked reptilian. They had large, scaly legs, clawed feet, and knotty fingers. Strong, leathery wings jutted from their backs, giving them a bird-like appearance.

I wasn't sure whether they were more human, reptile, or bird.

Half the flock carried bone-like clubs, while the other half had bows made of bone. Their weapons were of all different sizes and lengths, telling me they'd used many different types of victims to make each bow.

Egan walked beside me as we headed toward the dragons standing in the center of the neighborhood. The entire thunder was here.   •

Five other men with weapons came running toward us.

It looked like we had enough guns for everyone. There

were no children in the mix, so everyone was old enough to handle one.

"What's the plan?" a lady around the same age as Kayda asked. Determination filled her amethyst eyes, and she pulled her plum-brown hair into a ponytail. "Do we shift now?"

"No, Rose. Take a gun and hide. Worst case, we shift into our dragons, but their arrows can penetrate our scales. We need to stay human until we no longer can. The more of us we can group together, the better."

Draco stepped forward, taking control. "We can't stay circled like this, or they'll pick us off.

"You'll stay with them, right?" an older man asked. His thin gray hair barely covered his scalp, but his amber eyes held an intelligence that age couldn't diminish.

"Of course," Draco said and glanced at Ladon and Kayda, then Egan and me. "I'll stay with them."

Uh ... why are they so concerned about us? The odd wording had to mean something.

My dad is viewed as the youngest leader here. Egan stepped closer. "Let's move."

I looked over my shoulder, and the front line of harpies was now only several hundred yards away. Two at the front lifted their bows and pulled an arrow from the quiver they wore high on their backs above their wings.

"They're getting ready to shoot!" Draco yelled.

Our group ran in various directions.

Draco waved for us to follow him as he ran back to the house. He yelled, "We can shoot from the windows."

I ran as fast as I could to keep up with Egan beside me. The sound of flapping wings grew louder as the harpies caught up to us. We had to figure a way out of there.

An arrow whistled through the air, growing louder every second. At least one harpy was targeting us. I spun around to see who the target was, only to see an arrow heading straight for my head. "Duck!" I exclaimed to the others and rolled out of the way at the last possible second. The arrow landed only inches from where I'd been standing.

"Jade!" Egan cried with pure terror as he ran toward me. He grabbed me by the waist and threw me over his shoulder.

Each step he took jarred my body, but I ignored the pain and lifted my head. Twenty harpies veered off from the main group, racing after us.

Egan's home was a little ways away, and they were gaining on us. A harpy reloaded her bow and aimed right past us at the front of the group.

"Watch out!" I warned desperately. With the majority of the harpies after us, Vera's target was clear.

The arrow buzzed over our heads, and I heard a sickening thud. The iron smell of blood spilled into the air.

"Ladon!" Kayda whimpered.

"I'm fine," he grunted. "Keep going."

You need to put me down. Egan carrying me was slowing us down. *I'm fine.*

You stay right next to me, Egan said and paused to set me down.

As soon as my feet met solid earth, I sped toward the house.

Draco opened the door and waved us in. An arrow protruded from Ladon's upper shoulder, but he hadn't slowed down.

Thankfully, the wound looked superficial.

Egan's parents ran inside the house, and we were only a

few feet away. The harpies were so close I could hear them breathing.

The sound of another arrow being nocked sent a burst of adrenaline through me. I jumped the last few feet into the house and turned around.

Egan raced toward us, his face etched with pure determination. His golden eyes glowed as his dragon peeked through. Right as he crossed the threshold, an arrow followed, buzzing directly at my head. Shocked, I stood frozen in place.

"Move," Draco growled. He slammed the door shut and locked it.

A thud pounded where the arrow had hit the door instead of my brain. I stumbled back and sagged against the wall. My brain had short-circuited as I glanced at the warrior dragon. "Thank you."

"Don't thank me yet." He rushed into the smaller doorway. "Egan, I need your help. Jade, make sure no one gets through that door."

Of course, he'd leave me with the easy job. I crossed my arms, frowning at the locked wooden door. Did Draco expect them to float through it? Vera was strong, but I doubted she was that powerful.

Something loud pounded on the door, startling me.

What the hell was that?

It sounded again and again. Soon, there were multiple hard knocks on the door.

Holy shit, the harpies with the clubs were trying to break through.

Their noise grew louder as they attacked together. The door shook from the magnitude of the force.

"Uh ... guys." Now I understood why Draco had asked me to stay there. "We have a problem."

I placed my hands on the door to reinforce the wood. Each hit against the door jerked my entire body.

The noise turned into one continuous roar as more harpies joined the barrage. The hinges shook, and the door lurched hard against the metal. "Guys!" I yelled again.

"We're coming," Draco said, barely audible over all the noise.

I wasn't sure how much longer I could hold this. I was clueless about how many were on the other side of the door. They began clawing into the wood, determined to get in.

"Move," a loud voice crowed. "I'll get us through."

Something slammed into the door, and I flew back against the wall.

CHAPTER TWENTY-ONE

H itting the wall knocked the breath out of me, and I fell in a heap on the floor. The door swung open, and ten angry harpies attempted to get in at once, climbing over each other, desperate to get to me first.

"Keep low," Draco commanded as gunshots fired.

A harpy fell, but the others didn't care. Their eyes were glued to me like they had the overwhelming urge to hurt me.

A war cry pierced my ears as a harpy barreled through the others, her club held high over her head. She swung the bone downward, but a bullet pierced her chest. Her eyes widened, and she stumbled forward then fell, landing right on top of me. Her boobs plopped on my face, and her dirty hair acted like a shield between fresh air and her rancid smell. Warm blood trickled from her chest down my cheeks.

This was worse than any nightmare I'd ever had. Her body convulsed, jiggling her breasts. I felt a serious need to get her off me. Granted, I bet some guys in the world would've loved to be in my position.

I pushed her off me as an arrow plunged into the

harpy's side, right where my arm had been. The harpy groaned and flopped on the ground, blood pooling at the corners of her mouth.

My focus darted back to the door. Three harpies had their bows drawn and pointed at me. The ones with the clubs banged on the wood outside, adding fear to an already horrible situation.

This was how I imagined impending doom sounded.

A dragon roared as he flew into view, his dark scales reflecting the rising sun. He darted toward the harpies focused on me. Fire poured from his mouth, lighting up the strange women.

"Protect the royal family!" a person yelled, but I couldn't see who it was with all the harpies standing in my way. "They're attacking their home."

The dragon froze, flames pouring in the same spot, seemingly surprised by the news.

The front door of the house next to us opened, and a man around Ladon's age popped his head out, his hair askew. He stepped out of the house with a rifle. "The royal family lives here?"

Of course, the royal family would live here. We'd led Vera straight to the top. Surely Egan would've told me that if he'd known. We would have been extra cautious coming back.

The dragon shook his head like he was coming to, and the harpies dropped their clubs and ran inside the house, desperate to escape the flames the dragon spewed at anything that came close.

Their screams drowned out the rest of the conversation the two dragon shifters were having.

If we hadn't been fighting for our lives, it would've been

an amazing sight, but we had far more important things to focus on.

As they reached the threshold, Draco appeared beside me and fired at them one by one. A few took flight.

There was no telling where they were going. I'd moved to stand when Egan's large arms encircled me and pulled me farther into the house.

They're getting away. I tried squirming out of his hold.

Just give me a second. He raced us to the couch and set me down gently on the soft material.

I looked over his shoulder to find Ladon and Kayda kneeling in front of an open window in the middle of the room, shooting at the harpies trying to get inside that way.

Egan cupped my face. "Where are you hurt?"

His concern pulled my attention back to him. He'd asked me that same question more often than I'd have liked to admit. "I'm fine. It's the harpy's blood." If Roxy had been here, she'd have said something to the tune of, "Oh, the one you copped a feel of," defusing some of the tension. A laugh would've been nice right now.

"Thank God." Egan dropped his hands and clenched them into fists. "We wanted to get the wooden kitchen table in front of the door, but they broke through before we could get there."

Gunshots continued to fire as screams echoed all around.

"It's bad out there." I shivered. "Some dragons are shifting to fight in beast form."

"That's good." Egan faced his parents. "A mix is probably ideal considering how bad the situation is getting."

"This is insane." Kayda reloaded her gun and aimed out the window again. "It's like they have no fear."

I had a feeling that was the case. "Did you know the royal family lives here?" From what Egan had said, only a handful of people knew who they were. I was curious if his father did since he was considered a leader. "Apparently, that family is being attacked hard. Vera must know who they are."

"Wait." Egan tensed and straightened. "The royal family is here? You'd think that would have been brought up before the attack."

At least, he hadn't known. That made me feel better because I'd hoped he would've shared something like that with me.

"Yes, they're here," Ladon snapped, his focus on fighting the enemy that kept coming. The arrow had been removed from his shoulder, and fresh blood made his shirt cling to his back.

"Are you okay to fight?" I asked Ladon with concern. Here Egan was, all paranoid about me when his father was actually wounded.

"It's superficial." He nodded at me, his golden eyes lightening. "I'm completely fine to fight. Once we get through this, I'll get it bandaged."

Glass broke upstairs. The harpies had made it into the house.

"They need to know," Kayda scolded, aiming her gun at the stairs. "Do not try to change the subject."

Okay, I was done being helpless. I pulled my gun from my holster and ran to stand next to Ladon. These suckers had to be multiplying. It had looked like there were only a hundred or so earlier, but their numbers must have doubled. I pointed my gun and fired at the closest harpy.

"Need to know what?" Egan hurried next to his mom and pointed his rifle up the stairs. "Who are the royals? There's no point keeping it a secret now."

"Dammit." Ladon fired again and looked at Egan. "This wasn't how I wanted to tell you, but you and Jade must make it out of here alive. You two are the next king and queen of the dragons."

"What?" Egan stilled, and his breathing tensed. "Is this a sick joke?"

Loud tapping noises drew closer as harpies descended the stairs. For whatever reason, they were running down the stairs instead of flying. My mind was reeling from this brand-new information Ladon had unleashed on us. *This can't be real.*

Unfortunately, I think it is. Egan kept his aim at the stairwell as the harpies came flooding down. There were at least ten lined up on the stairs while three flew overhead. They came fast and hard.

Us being the future king and queen of the dragons was something we'd have to deal with later. Our focus needed to be on survival.

Between the shriek of harpies and the gunfire, my ears rang. I shot round after round, my hands shaking even after the gun had stopped vibrating. They were closing in.

Draco hadn't come back around, and I hoped that was a good thing. They hadn't come through the doorway, which could only mean that Draco was still alive and fighting.

Four dragons in varying colors of green swarmed straight toward us.

The largest one had glowing amber eyes that contrasted against its fern-colored- scales. It led the group to the harpies attacking us.

Harpies with clubs flew to intercept them and attacked. At least, we had backup, but we needed more.

I wanted to pay attention to their fight, but I couldn't. A harpy flew in front of the window and nocked an arrow. She released the arrow, and it sailed straight toward us.

Ladon was too preoccupied with shooting at the closer harpies to see the looming threat. Not knowing what else to do, I lunged at him, praying the gun didn't go off. I sacked him, my arms going around his waist, and landed right on top of him.

The arrow lodged into my upper thigh. I reached down and clutched the bone, and blinding pain overcame me. "What the ..." It hurt worse than I would've ever imagined. My eyes watered.

"We've got to get that out of her leg. Egan! Ladon! Shoot!" Kayda turned her back on the increasing number of attackers coming down the stairs.

Ladon gently rolled me off him as a harpy flew in through the window. He grabbed the gun and used the butt to knock her back outside before turning it around and firing again.

The pain throbbed up my leg. My leg jerked, making the pain worse, so I clutched it, trying to hold my leg steady.

Kayda grabbed the fletching of the arrow that protruded from my leg.

"What are you doing? You aren't supposed to remove an arrow," I whispered and tried jerking away from her, but she held on tight.

"We have to get this out. It's laced with fae poison. It'll be worse if we don't pull it out," she replied and yanked.

The intense pain doubled me over, and I puked all over their floor. Under normal circumstances, I'd have been embarrassed, but this situation had put things into perspective. If puking was the worst thing that happened to me, I was doing better than most.

"Jade." Egan looked at me. "Baby ..."

That endearment always caught me off guard.

"I understand you're concerned, but you need to focus on the winged hags or your mate will get hurt worse," Kayda scolded as she examined my wound.

Surprisingly, the pain receded by removing that damn arrow. More blood came out, but it didn't hurt as badly. "Wow, you were right. The pain is manageable this way."

"They coat their spears in something that intensifies pain. So Ladon struggled more than he admitted earlier when he'd been hit. The bleeding isn't too worrisome, and it's pushing the poison out of your system. You should be good, but take it easy on the leg."

"How do you know all this?" I asked.

"I was a nurse for a couple of years before finding Ladon." She held up her gun and raced over to Egan just as a harpy hit him in the head with the club.

He stumbled backward before catching himself, and his mother shot the harpy in the chest.

We had to find a way out of the house. There were too many harpies attacking us. I linked to Egan. *I'm going to check on Draco.*

I rose to my feet and glanced back. The three of them were holding off the harpies, but I needed to hurry before they overpowered us again. We might not be able to recover a second time.

Refusing to limp, I walked slower than normal. The bleeding was already slowing, reminding me that I wasn't fully human anymore. A nice perk about being a dragon shifter was quicker healing.

As I turned into the entryway, I prepared myself for the worst-case scenarios. I'd expected harpies to be flooding the house, but Draco fought outside the door with a few dragons attacking the harpies. The harpies tried to go around the dragons and attack us from the windows. Maybe splitting up hadn't been the best decision. "Guys, we need help."

I stepped outside. Fifty harpies were fighting the other dragons, but the rest were focused on us. Now I understood why—Vera wanted to take out the royal family.

"What do you mean?" Draco asked, and his eyes locked on my wound. "What happened?"

"Most of them are attacking from the back." Draco obviously thought he was protecting us, and I couldn't blame him. He hadn't expected a horde to be trying to get inside through the back windows. *Egan, there are a lot fewer out front. It's our best way out.*

They're gaining ground. We'll be out there in a second.

Draco's eyes widened. "Why? Unless the witch figured out you're part of the royal family and is targeting you."

"That's what I'm thinking." I wanted to blame Mindy, but if Egan hadn't known, how could she? The way she'd pushed too hard despite Egan having found his fated mate had me suspicious of her intentions.

"Protect her!" Draco called to the two nearby dragons and ran into the house to help my mate.

The two dragons flew toward me, and around ten harpies flew around the house. They gazed at me, and I swore one of them smirked.

They must have heard Draco and decided to check out who he was talking about.

A shrill cackle escaped one, though I couldn't tell which. The harpy that had smirked lifted her bow and arrow, aiming it at me.

My dragon surged forward into my mind. Between my injured leg and my dragon's desperate need to take control, I didn't fight back. Instead, I chose to trust her.

The clothes ripped from my body as I shifted within seconds. Just as the harpy released the arrow, I took to the sky.

Something hot built inside as I flew at her. It unnerved me how each one looked identical at a glance, but I couldn't waste time inspecting them to see whether that was true. Survival was of the utmost importance.

The harpy drew her bow, but I gained ground on her.

I felt heat bubbling inside me, and my dragon pushed it from deep inside my belly. Flames and smoke spewed from my mouth, charring her. As she dropped, no longer a threat, I held the flames in and spun around. Another archer reached for an arrow.

I've got you covered. Egan linked as he raised his gun and shot at a harpy behind me.

My dragon purred. For once, he wasn't trying to protect me or get me to stand down. He was treating me as an equal, and I loved it.

A harpy with a club lowered its head and flew at me, trying to distract me while the other one shot at me. I didn't know what to do or which one to choose. Either way, one of them would hurt me.

CHAPTER TWENTY-TWO

My eyes flicked from the archer harpy to the one charging at me like a bull with her bone club tucked at her side.

Ugh ... which one should I attack? That arrow in my leg had hurt like a son of a bitch, so I should take that one out. With the club, my body wouldn't be susceptible to the poison.

Unless ... I pulled something epic.

To achieve this level of awesomeness, the timing would have to align, but it was the best shot I had to avoid injury.

The harpy drew back her arrow as the bull-like one got within five feet of me. My heart raced, and I hoped I could pull this off.

"Jade!" Draco yelled with alarm from below.

He'd distract me if he kept that up. I now understood how lucky the wolves were to have a pack link. It would've come in handy with the thunder, but dragons didn't have that luxury, and wishing dragons had that was a waste of energy.

The harpy lifted the club over her shoulder like a softball player and aimed for my head. I waited a quick second before ducking and flying upward. She startled as I wrapped my arms around her waist and wings, trapping her.

The club fell, and she screamed and buried her face in my chest. This wasn't much better than the boobs. She tried to bite me, but her teeth couldn't pierce my scales, probably from the amount of decay.

I needed a bath desperately.

A whistle grew louder, and I watched as the other harpy had released the arrow. The poisoned-laced tip barreled straight toward my backside.

I had to move fast. I attempted to spin the harpy around, but she jerked, stalling my rotation. Dammit, these creatures were sturdier than I'd given them credit for. This might've been a bad idea.

Desperation clawed at me, and I tried to move her again, using every ounce of strength I had. With the arrow only inches away, I turned her enough so that it lodged into her back between her wings.

If I'd thought I'd heard their worst screams yet, boy did she prove me wrong. My eardrums felt like they would burst at the magnitude. I released her, and she tumbled to the ground. She flapped her wings, but they barely moved, probably from the pain.

Watch out. Egan linked, drawing my attention to him. He lifted his rifle as absolute terror filled his eyes.

I looked to where the barreled was pointed, and the harpy nocked her bow again. A sick, dark chuckle left her as she released the arrow.

Egan's hand jolted, and a bullet launched from the barrel. My ears rang from the harpy's scream, the gunshot barely audible.

The bullet lodged in the harpy's shoulder, causing her to convulse as she released the arrow. Egan didn't hesitate to fire at her again, and he hit her right in the heart. She fell.

The arrow didn't come close to hitting me and landed several yards away to where no one stood.

Realizing we were no longer in the house, the horde headed straight for us.

"We need to get you to safety!" Draco yelled and turned to a couple of dragons in human form. "Tell the others that plans have changed. Everyone needs to come out and fight. Half should shift, and the other half should stay human to fire the rifles. The harpies don't plan to split, and we need everyone in the fight."

"Yes, sir!" a guy who didn't look much older than us yelled and ran in the opposite direction, toward the houses at the other end.

Fifty harpies moved together toward us, their eyes locked on Egan and his parents. It scared me that the identity of the king was no longer secret. The way they were dead set on Egan's family and me screamed that our cover as regular shifters was blown. But we'd have to sort out the implications later when we were safe and sound.

Draco's jaw twitched, and displeasure wafted off him. "I thought they would have spread across the entire village and not just focused on your home and the ones near it."

From a strategic perspective, I would've thought the same thing. No one could've guessed that they'd know who the royal family was when only a handful, if even that many, in the thunder knew.

"Egan, when the group gets here, we need to split off when most of the harpies are engaged in battle," Draco commanded as if he were the ruler. "You all need to shift. It'll be harder to distinguish you in beast form. But wait until they're preoccupied. It's bad enough that they might know what Jade looks like in animal form."

Egan lifted his chin, anger fueling his movements. "We can't leave our people to fight while we run and hide."

I wished I were standing beside my mate, but if the harpies didn't recognize me since they hadn't been around here when I'd shifted, I didn't need to give myself away.

"It's more important that you survive this," Draco told Egan. "You and your family are the only ones preventing the fae dragon from taking control of this realm too."

How could he know? The dragon was in an entirely different realm. The threat didn't sound that real even though I wasn't a huge fan of anyone dying.

Remember, harpies are from the fae realm. Egan scratched the back of his neck as he gazed at me. *Which means the fae dragon is involved. We've been hiding from him for centuries.*

"Son, he's right." Ladon raised his gun at the horde. "You two have to survive."

Egan snapped his head in his father's direction. "You're the king—"

Ladon shot his gun at the harpies that were within range, cutting Egan's words off.

Kayda followed her husband's lead and fired into the cluster of harpies.

"Kill as many as you can," Draco said and gestured to Egan's gun.

The four of them took down several women flying straight at us. The threat of death didn't deter them, which was damn crazy. Any sane being would have run for their lives, telling me way too much about the fae realm.

Some of the archers stopped their forward trajectory

and flew higher into the sky, ready to fire down at us. For the first time, they ignored me as they drew their bows.

I had to do something before Egan and the others got hurt.

I flew forward, and Draco grumbled, "Holy shit. She's lost her fucking mind. What part of 'don't put yourself in harm's way' did she not understand? Balls!"

Despite hiding from the modern world for so long, he was pretty damn versed in the art of cursing. I'd thought people were better-mannered back then.

Egan linked with me, furious. *What are you doing? You're going to get yourself killed.*

I'm attacking the ones in the back that are focused on you. I didn't plan on taking out the ones with clubs. I let the fire build in my stomach, ready to spill it over those who attempted to fight me as I flew by.

The flapping of wings sounded behind me, and I turned to find ten dragons heading our way with men and women trailing behind them.

We were finally getting the backup we desperately needed. I turned around and flew toward the horde. Every three shots, a harpy fell, their numbers dwindling.

When I was ten feet from the others, the four dragons that had been fighting behind the house joined me, two flanking me on each side. Luckily, Egan and the others were able to shoot around them.

Despite not being able to communicate, we were all on the same page. Smoke trickled from their noses as they called on the flames inside them. As we met the horde of harpies, two of the dragons breathed flames over them while the two others and I flew underneath them, hiding under the masses to attack the three archers in the back.

Arrows whizzed as the three harpies attacked our thunder. I pushed my wings harder to reach the harpies before they could launch more arrows. The two dragons with me kept pace, and we shot upward toward the enemies.

I bit the reptilian leg of the one in the middle. My dragon wanted to gag at the overwhelming stench, and my stomach revolted, but I pushed it aside and jerked my head.

Losing all sense of control, the winged creature let out an ear-piercing scream, but I was partially deaf from the other harpy, or maybe more immune to their noises. Either way, I didn't want to claw my ears out, so that was a win.

Reaching up, I trapped her body with my arms and dug my talons into her wings. I slashed through her skin, and warm blood oozed from her injury.

Releasing her, I let her drop and spun around to check on the others. Between the four dragons that had attacked with me and the ten on their way, the fight began to look promising for us.

A faint breeze blew behind me, and I pivoted to find Egan a few feet away in dragon form. For all our sakes, I hoped no one realized who he was. I scolded him, *You were supposed to wait.*

As soon as the five of you attacked, their focus turned to you and the ten dragons. They didn't see me change, but dammit, do you know how hard it was to watch you from down there? His golden eyes narrowed.

If he wanted to make me feel bad, it wasn't happening. *Don't give me that. You were fighting on the ground. You were as likely to get hurt down there as up here.*

But not being beside you was driving me mad. He roared as a harpy flew at us, and he shot flames all over her body.

They aren't very bright.

Egan shook his dragon head. *No, they aren't. Come on, Draco and my parents are waiting.*

But ... I glanced back as more dragons came forward. The harpies were being slaughtered, and there wasn't much risk to the dragons.

Once we get out, we'll hide somewhere, and Draco will bring them to us. We need to relocate because one could escape and tell the others of our location. Egan nudged my body with his. *We wouldn't be leaving them if it wasn't under control. And Dad's right. If they capture us, it'll be worse for everyone.*

He was right, and we had taken the brunt of the attack. Hell, we'd done most of the fighting. *Okay. Let's go.* Maybe if they realized the royal family was gone, they'd retreat.

I followed Egan to a grassy hill that jutted from the edge of the cave. The other side wasn't visible from here.

As we approached, Egan landed next to the last house in the neighborhood. I mirrored his movements and noticed that the dragons were still gaining ground on the harpies. There was no way these fae creatures could win now, and none of them were paying attention to us.

Egan clutched my arm and we made it to the side of the house where the hill started a few feet to the right.

Let's hurry before someone catches us. Egan linked as he nudged me in front of him.

I ran as gently and quickly as possible to the other side. Draco snarled but stopped short when he smelled me ... or saw me.

What the hell? Why would he—then it hit me. You couldn't see shit from this side. But if we stayed quiet, no one would consider looking over here.

Ladon's dragon stood as tall as Egan's, and his scales were a dark army green. Kayda was a few inches shorter than me, and her scales were a shade lighter than Ladon's.

The two of them took off, leading the way to the secret passageway only they knew about.

Egan reached my side, and Draco waved us forward, wanting to take the rear.

That was fine, but even if it hadn't been, we couldn't argue without making noise and giving away our position.

We ran along the grass, keeping our steps as quiet as possible. The light gray stone of the cave sat to the right with the grass to the left. Farther up, the greenery grew more sparse and the ground more rocky.

If I'd been in my human form, my feet would have gotten cut, but in this sturdier form, I might as well have been walking on a cloud. Well, okay, that was a stretch, but it didn't hurt.

At the top of the hill, the cave was covered with a series of stacked rocks, with green moss growing all over it. It was thick and growing through the crevices.

This was what Ladon must have meant when he'd said it probably wasn't passable, but with our talons, surely we could make it through.

I moved to attack one side, then felt an all too familiar tickle at the base of my neck. I stilled, and my heart stopped. *Egan, she's here.*

CHAPTER TWENTY-THREE

The tingling increased as Vera's presence drew closer. How the hell had she gotten here? She couldn't walk through the entrance to the cave.

Egan spun away from the escape route. We stood side by side, staring down the threat as Ladon and Kayda worked to remove the vines.

The warrior dragon tilted his head in confusion, then the rancid smell of harpy hit. He stood protectively in front of us, preparing to fight.

The foul smell told me how Vera had gotten here. The fae creatures were working with her as her personal chauffeur. The stench grew stronger. I shuddered and wiped my dragon face where blood had dripped from the boobful of convulsing harpy.

A harpy flew over the hill, Vera dangling from its talons, confirming what I'd suspected. Vera's stringy caramel hair looked clean for once as it blew in the breeze but especially compared to the half-human carrying her. Her eyes were as black as night and locked on Egan and me.

"Lower me to the ground," Vera commanded.

The winged creature obliged, slowly placed her on the ground, and stepped behind the witch.

Irritated, I wished I were in human form so I could tell the bitch off.

"Well, well, what do we have here?" Vera wore her standard Star Wars t-shirt. The only thing missing was her thick glasses that usually framed her face.

The stench of harpies warned me that she had backup. *Egan, there are more near.*

I smell them too, Egan said with disgust.

Not wanting to waste any time, I took a menacing step toward her. The horrible woman needed to die before she hurt anyone else.

She lifted a hand and grinned. "I wouldn't be so eager. I want to say a few things first. After all, don't you want to understand why?"

Two harpies holding bows appeared with smug expressions.

None of us had guns, and the harpies were out of range of our flames. They could shoot at us before we ever got near. We needed to come up with a plan, but the only person I could communicate with was Egan.

Draco lifted his wings like he was preparing to cover us, and Egan's parents moved to stand beside their son.

We were trapped, so we'd have to play along with Vera's game until an opportunity to run or fight opened up. *Any ideas on how to get out of this? We'll have to kill her or she'll track us to the new location.*

Not yet. And you're right. We have to end this or she'll keep hunting us. Egan's dragon was so stiff he looked like a statue.

The danger we were in was unreal. For a moment, I'd thought we were going to come out of this mostly unscathed. This was what I got for my wishful thinking.

"So this is the royal family." Vera tapped her crusty fingers against her lips.

I cringed. I wouldn't be putting my fingers anywhere near my mouth after being near those harpies. At least, I'd been in my beast form when I'd bitten the harpy's leg, but the act had still made me sick.

"I'm disappointed it was this easy to get you." Vera sighed, and her shoulders sagged. "But it's fine. My centuries-old grudge still makes this moment worthwhile."

I blew out a breath, unable to hold back my reaction. Trixie had nailed the fact that Vera was either very old or more pure-blooded than most witches. I wondered how old she actually was.

She chuckled and tilted her head. "Are you surprised? I had to sacrifice a lot to make it this long without dwindling my power."

Draco growled at the implication. Obviously, he had a better idea of what that meant than I did.

What am I missing?

For a witch to live that long without giving up their power means they sacrificed someone they love. In other words, they gave up their humanity for revenge.

The magnitude of the meaning hit me. Who had she sacrificed to achieve this?

"Aw, even in beast form, I can see your disgust," Vera sneered and paced in front of us. "But you see, my five-year-old daughter deserved it. After all, she was the reason Blaize met his fated mate that day in the village."

Five? Now I really felt sick and had more reason to end the bitch.

She paused, letting the information wash over us. Her

eyes hazed over each one of us, enjoying whatever she found.

"Egan, your great, great grandfather and I were in love." Her face wrinkled with pain as she frowned. "Well, before he met *her*," she spat.

When this was over, I'd have to catch up on his family lineage. Most girls dreamed of being a princess, but so far, my entire experience with it made Hell sound like an amusement park.

"He found his mate the same day we attended a village event. He didn't want to go; rumors floated that the fae dragon king was growing displeased because even though your family had left the realm, his family could never become the true leaders over the dragons. The fae king's magic wasn't strong enough, and none of the other fae races respected them as much. However, my daughter demanded to go to the event, and Blaize gave in. He loved her as if she were his own." She clenched her hands at her sides. "Her father died within a year of her birth, and the two of them connected."

She didn't sound happy about their bond. Not every man would've connected with a child that wasn't his own, especially back then.

"Within the first hour, he saw his mate. I felt the change in him." She rubbed her arms like she was cold. "When he told me he could no longer be with me, I killed my daughter in front of him. It was the only way I could truly hurt him. When he tried to stop me, I disappeared and watched him mourn my child's death. Then I began my mission. My true calling. I found a fae man who put me in contact with the king, and we planned to ruin Blaize's life like he'd ruined mine."

She'd been a heartless bitch even back then. What kind

of mother could kill her own child? She practically glowed from the memory.

"I helped the fae dragon king hunt down the other dragons." The corners of her mouth tilted upward. "Kind of like now."

She was a completely miserable person who wanted those around her to be worse off, and I realized we were up against someone that had nothing to lose. This wasn't a granddaughter following in her grandmother's footsteps; this witch had lived longer than Egan and his parents. She was completely delusional and hell-bent on revenge. The amount of hatred she'd carried all these years was something most would never understand.

"You're probably asking yourself how I couldn't find you until now." She laughed like she'd told a joke. "But I'll answer your burning question first. I killed Blaize and his mate but wasn't aware they'd had a child before I got to them. When the dragons went into true hiding, cutting themselves off completely from the outside world, and the full power didn't transfer to the fae dragon, I realized I'd greatly miscalculated. I might have killed the man I loved, but his child with *her* lived on, and I couldn't allow that. However, I couldn't locate them since I had no other dragon's blood or possessions to track. I'd killed too fast."

She's wrapping this up. From everything I'd watched and read, after villains wrapped up their spiels, they got to the action. Unfortunately, this was real life, and killing us was high on her priority list.

The two harpies remained focused on us, even though Vera had a crazed look. A victorious smile spread across her face, making her look creepier than the creatures trapping us. "But today, I get my revenge and, in a way, get retribution for Mindy. After all, she and I have a lot in common and bonded over the thought of Jade's death. Mindy let it slip that a former human shouldn't become queen. Of course, I had to agree and was thrilled that she'd confirmed what I'd suspected. The prince was allowed to leave the thunder in search of his mate to continue the royal lineage."

Great, psycho bitch and Mindy had bonded. That sounded about right.

When this goes down, get behind me. Egan inched slightly in front.

Yeah, that wasn't happening, but I had to play along. I didn't want to reveal my objective of not listening quite yet. He'd do something more dangerous before I could. *You're the blood heir. It makes sense—*

And you wouldn't be part of this life if it wasn't for me, Egan said loudly, hurting my ears. He growled deeply, his entire body quaking.

He'd never cut me off before. Shocked didn't even describe what I was feeling. I was teetering between amused, offended, horrified, and surprised. Laughter bubbled out, but it sounded like I was choking in this form.

Vera squinted at me. "What's your problem?"

The harpies zeroed in on me, expecting me to attack.

Okay, I hadn't planned on this, but I'd take it.

Jade, I swear … Egan groaned. *You're a magnet for trouble.*

That I couldn't disagree with, but since I had their attention, I'd use it to our advantage. I took a large step forward. A harpy hissed and drew her arrow.

"I'd be a little more careful if I were you." Vera waggled her brows, and not in a sexy way. "I may have to hurt someone you love."

She was already threatening to hurt Egan and my new family. Who else could she have?

Vera whistled, and two more harpies came into view, one holding a horrified Mindy, but my heart stuttered when I saw who the second one held.

My mother dangled from their talons, blood dripping down her arm and onto the ground. Her brown eyes were wide with fear, and her brown hair was soaked with deep crimson.

My heart sank. How did they know who she was? And how long had the witch had her? Even though she wasn't involved in my life, I couldn't lose another parent.

Everything inside me screamed to save her. I rushed toward her as Vera bounced on the balls of her feet.

"Yes, feel the panic and terror." Vera cackled. "Do you think you can get to her in time?"

The sheer joy in her voice turned my blood to ice.

Jade! Egan linked, his anxiety pushing mine past my breaking point.

This bitch was unpredictable and wanted to hurt us. I soared into the sky, desperate to get to Mom.

"I guess we'll find out!" Vera yelled gleefully. "Let her mother go."

I roared as the harpy released my mom, letting her tumble to her death.

ABOUT THE AUTHOR

Jen L. Grey is a *USA Today* Bestselling Author who writes Paranormal Romance, Urban Fantasy, and Fantasy genres.

Jen lives in Tennessee with her husband, two daughters, and two miniature Australian Shepherd. Before she began writing, she was an avid reader and enjoyed being involved in the indie community. Her love for books eventually led her to writing. For more information, please visit her website and sign up for her newsletter.

Check out my future projects and book signing events at my website.
www.jenlgrey.com

ALSO BY JEN L. GREY

The Hidden King Trilogy

Dragon Mate

Dragon Heir

Dragon Queen

The Wolf Born Trilogy

Hidden Mate

Blood Secrets

Awakened Magic

The Marked Wolf Trilogy

Moon Kissed

Chosen Wolf

Broken Curse

Wolf Moon Academy Trilogy

Shadow Mate

Blood Legacy

Rising Fate

The Royal Heir Trilogy

Wolves' Queen

Wolf Unleashed

Wolf's Claim

Bloodshed Academy Trilogy

Year One

Year Two

Year Three

The Half-Breed Prison Duology (Same World As Bloodshed Academy)

Hunted

Cursed

The Artifact Reaper Series

Reaper: The Beginning

Reaper of Earth

Reaper of Wings

Reaper of Flames

Reaper of Water

Stones of Amaria (Shared World)

Kingdom of Storms

Kingdom of Shadows

Kingdom of Ruins

Kingdom of Fire

The Pearson Prophecy

Dawning Ascent

Enlightened Ascent

Reigning Ascent

Stand Alones

Death's Angel

Rising Alpha

Printed in Great Britain
by Amazon

67756581R00137